SPELLED
Amethyst Book One
Kate St. Clair

This book is a work of fiction. Names, characters, places and incidents are products of the author's imagination or are used fictitiously. Any resemblance to actual events or locales or persons, living or dead, is entirely coincidental.

Copyright © 2014 by Kate St. Clair

All rights reserved, including the right to reproduce this book or portions thereof in any form whatsoever. For further information, please contact: info@blackhillpress.com

ISBN-13: 978-0615962023
ISBN-10: 0615962025

Edited by Ryan Gattis
Artwork by Davide Bonazzi

Printed in the U.S.A.

BLACK HILL PRESS
blackhillpress.com

Black Hill Press is a publishing collective founded on collaboration. Our growing family of writers and artists are dedicated to the novella—a distinctive, often overlooked literary form that offers the focus of a short story and the scope of a novel. We believe a great story is never defined by its length.

Our independent press produces uniquely curated collections of Contemporary American Novellas. We also celebrate innovative paperback projects with our Special Editions series. Books are available in both print and digital formats, online and in your local bookstore, library, museum, university gift shop, and selected specialty accounts. Discounts are available for book clubs and teachers.

Contemporary American Novellas
1. Corrie Greathouse, *Another Name for Autumn*
2. Ryan Gattis, *The Big Drop: Homecoming*
3. Jon Frechette, *The Frontman*
4. Richard Gaffin, *Oneironautics*
5. Ryan Gattis, *The Big Drop: Impermanence*
6. Alex Sargeant, *Sci-Fidelity*
7. Veronica Bane, *Mara*
8. Kevin Staniec, *Begin*
9. Arianna Basco, *Palms Up*
10. Douglas Cowie, *Sing for Life: Tin Pan Alley*
11. Tomas Moniz, *Bellies and Buffalos*
12. Brett Arnold, *Avalon, Avalon*
13. Douglas Cowie, *Sing for Life: Away, You Rolling River*

14. Pam Jones, *The Biggest Little Bird*
15. Peppur Chambers, *Harlem's Awakening*
16. Kate St. Clair, *Spelled*
17. Veronica Bane, *Miyuki*
18. William Brandon, *Silence*

Special Editions
1. Kevin Staniec, *29 to 31: A Book of Dreams*

Halloween

"I need to tell you about the Sagestone fire," he says, his voice rasping like each word is being scraped out of him. "I need you to know how this started."

My eyelids are too heavy to open. I try but it's like two thumbs are resting on top of them, holding them down. I can't do anything but lie there and see the hallway of the old high school emerge from the fog in my mind's eye. It surrounds me, makes me feel like I'm standing there, two months ago exactly. I shiver when he tells me Keir chose the place because he knew it'd be empty, and he knew how to get in.

"The boy, Matthew Townsend," he goes on, "was dead when I got there."

Every word adds a brushstroke to the scene until it's as clear as my own memory. It's the spell that's doing it. I can feel it crouching in the back of my brain like a gargoyle, watching the vision unfold while I'm powerless to do anything to stop it, change it, making it *real*.

I can see the hallway of the old school, everything washed in the grey darkness of nighttime. His feet, *my feet*, send echoes circling off the walls as I follow the faint smell of smoke down the hall. When I stop outside of French room 2B, my hands reach out and open the door.

The fire Keir started is on the floor, singeing the slip-resistant linoleum in the middle of a black casting circle. Desks sit clustered around it. Matthew's body is slung across the long table in the corner. Seeing him there, so rigid and still, makes my throat close until I almost can't breathe.

The door shuts behind me, drawing Keir's attention away from the embers.

What took you so long? He says as he snatches a knife off the floor and tosses it at me, hilt first. My hands barely manage to snag the handle.

Get his blood, Keir says, sliding a ceramic bowl across the floor until it knocks into my shoe. *We'll do you first.*

My body draws near to Matthew, and I want so badly to open my eyes, break through this nightmare. I watch my hand guide the knife to Matthew's grey-blue skin and split it in a line. There's fingerprint-shaped bruises darkening along his neck.

"Keir strangled him before I got there," he says. "Just before."

He's dead, but Matthew's eyes don't seem vacant yet, like some part of him is digging his nails in, refusing to be torn out.

The ceramic bowl in my hands catches the blood that flows down Matthew's elbow.

His voice shakes when he says, "Lifeblood had to come from an artery. Keir taught me that. The heart was best, but I just couldn't put the knife between Matthew's ribs, dead or not."

My hands hold out the bowl to Keir and he takes it, mixing a fistful of ashes into it, something like pigment powder. He holds the mixture over the fire, speaking in guttural words that don't sound like any language I've heard before. The darkness deepens in the room, as if it's being called, clustering in the corners like silent observers.

Keir digs in his backpack and pulls out a pen, just a regular ballpoint that's been emptied of its ink, but it has a needle on its end. I sit in front of him, horrified as I gather my shirt up at the back of my neck. Keir goes to work, dipping into the rust-colored paste and piercing a stinging pattern into my back.

"I knew how wrong it was," he says. "I knew I was breaking a part of myself that I'd never fix again. It's hard to explain. Each puncture kind of felt like there was a wholeness filling me. Like all my life I'd been half empty, you know? I couldn't keep going like that. I'd rather be someone else, and let this other side take over, than deal with being an unfinished person. I never really thought of stopping. Not even once."

In the room, Keir works the makeshift needle down to my lower back.

Almost done, Keir says, his voice strained with the effort of keeping his hand steady. *The last mark is tricky.*

As soon as he's done saying it, the fire in the middle of the room bursts like a mushroom cloud, stretching up in fury up to the speckled white ceiling. The Mineral fiber tiles take up the flames like gasoline, and the whole room looses its breath and starts to choke.

"I knew it was Matthew," he says, "driving the fire with all the hatred and anger for us that was too strong to move on, leave the place where his life had been stolen."

The pen drops from Keir's hand, skittering across the floor. We're both on our feet, running for the door. The handle is jammed, swollen with the heat. We try the windows, but the metal burns our hands.

"Matthew trapped us," he says. "His final revenge."

I grab a chair and break it across a window, chipping out a hole in the glass the size of a dime. It takes six more tries to smash a gap big enough to fit us. I scrape my body through as shards tear at my elbows. When I'm almost out, still hanging onto the windowsill, I turn back to Keir, but he's not behind me. He's running to the body, refusing to leave it.

As soon as Keir touches Matthew's skin, the fire retaliates, eating up every molecule of air left in the room before exploding out the windows. Heat surges into my nose and mouth, burning down my throat, as I hurl myself to the grass outside. After that, I drag my body across the parking lot, collapsing behind an electrical box.

"Sagestone High," he tells me, "was gone before the fire trucks even got there. I didn't think there was any way Keir could've gotten out. All the evidence was wiped away by the fire. I thought it was some kind of gift. A second chance almost. I walked away after that. To this day, I've never once looked at the tattoos on my back."

That's what he says, anyway. I feel the spell loosing its hold on me. My vision clears, like a gentle wind sweeping the fog away, and I open my eyes.

It's just me now, in my own body, still stuck in my hospital bed, and him in the chair beside me. He leans forward, pressing the heels of his hands into his eye sockets like it hurts him too much to see me.

Something's just been lost between us. I can feel our innocence draining from the room, and a dark weight settling in its place.

"If you'd told me one day ago," I say, "we might have been able to save you."

Two Months Earlier

"I hate this day," my younger sister Charlotte says, slamming the passenger side door. Her green eyes glower at me amidst several layers of eyeliner, flecks of emerald set in coal. The littered floor of my car rattles against our feet as we wait for our brother and sister to come outside.

"You're fantastic in the morning," I say, patting Charlotte on the head.

She swats me hard.

"Everything is going to be different," she huffs. "They didn't ask us if we wanted to mingle with all of Sagestone's rejects."

"They aren't rejects, they're relief students. They had to go to school somewhere." I run my thumbs over the peeling beige leather on the steering wheel, unable to quiet the fluttering of excitement in my chest. "We're all nervous. First day of school is always big."

"I don't care enough to be nervous," she scoffs. She piles her dark chocolate hair into a nondescript bun as if to prove her disinterest.

"This is a good development." Charlotte's twin Callie heaves herself up into the backseat by the seatbelt. She's wearing a dress we bought the day before. We share the idea that new clothes are like blank slates, no previous influence. Thus, any big occasion required new clothes. My father does not agree, but that's men for you.

"Wellsey needed more guys," Callie goes on. "Our selection did not profit from puberty."

"Wyatt will probably disagree." I roll down the window. "Wyatt! Come on!" I shout toward our house.

Our fourteen-year-old brother slams the front door. His backpack and two duffle bags knock against his legs the whole way down the drive, making him walk like a drunk.

"Dad's taking Abby to school," he says, stuffing his gear into the backseat, much of it directly on top of Callie.

"Oh good. We might actually be on time," I say, putting the car in gear. Cutting the drive to the middle school shaves off a good ten minutes. The ancient SUV rocks forward, jostling its passengers.

"Hey! Get down!" Callie bellows. She beats her hand against the window, directing her order toward our house, where her grey and white cat is perched on the roof.

"Jeez, Callie, roll down the freaking window," Wyatt says, doing it for her.

She thrusts her whole top half out, unleashing a tirade at the cat until we turn the corner. Ruby ticks her ears back, but grudgingly starts picking her way down the shingles.

Callie pulls her head back in, leaning forward and brushing out my long hair with her fingers.

"You didn't wear the headband I picked out for you," she pouts as she says it.

"Nope," I say, recalling the neon red, bow-adorned monstrosity she had cooed over. Our school was absorbing half the students from Sagestone, I didn't need to look like a lobster on our first day.

The overcrowding is evident as soon as we enter the school. The noise of pre-class chatter, usually a gentle hum, is almost deafening now. Charlotte and I look at each other.

"It's a little loud," she practically shouts.

"Something definitely seems different," I jokingly agree.

Wyatt unshackles himself from us, heading for the freshmen wing. Taylor Fitsch shoves a new girl out of the way to get to me, wrapping me in a hug.

"Georgia!" she says. "It's a madhouse in here. I wonder if there's even going to be seats for everyone. "Whoa," Taylor says, her gaze landing somewhere behind me. Her wide blue eyes look almost hungry. "Check him out."

I snort and glance over my shoulder, expecting to see some hulking jock, Taylor's type. But that's not what I see.

There is an angel in the hallway. He's tall, with jet-black hair and the buttery brown skin half-Hispanic kids come by naturally. I can only see his profile at first, but he turns to talk to someone else and cracks a smile. My body can't decide if it wants to admit it likes him, or get me out of that walkway. His chin and nose are perfectly proportioned, I can't deny that, but there's a darkness in his face that makes my stomach clench. So serious for someone so young. Taylor's hand closes around my arm.

"I need to meet him," she says, dragging me in his direction.

I try to plant my feet.

"Wait, what?" I splutter. The idea of being thrust into conversation with this guy before I've regained my wits is not ideal.

Taylor yanks me forward, her sinewy arms overpowering me. "Come on, he's just a guy."

As we near, Alison Holmes comes into view across from him. She smoothes her glossy blonde hair and smiles, working her magic. Now this seems like even less of a good idea.

We stop right beside Alison and the guy, drawing their attention. Alison stabs us with a glare, her lips plastered over her square teeth. The guy regards Taylor good-naturedly, clearly not aware of the awkwardness he's just been thrust into.

"They didn't say we were getting students from Bratton Academy," Taylor says to him.

I groan softly. Bratton is the teen modeling and acting academy in Austin. He chuckles, the tiniest hint of red lacing his cheeks. It softens him just enough to take the sharp edge off his appearance.

"Sorry, no such luck," the guy says. His voice is low, moving fluidly from one word to the next like water over rocks.

I find myself longing to hear him speak again.

"I'm Taylor, by the way," she asserts, sticking her hand out. The guy shakes it, and I think Alison might tackle her right there.

"I'm Luke Caulfield," the guy says.

"And that's Georgia." Taylor turns to me. "Don't stand behind me like a freak, Gee."

She practically shoves me into Luke and I look up at him, my tongue locking onto the roof of my mouth. His eyes are the most vibrant blue I've ever seen, standing out from his tan skin like water in cupped hands. But a strange hardness edges them too. They're the kind of eyes that always know something you don't.

He knits his brow just slightly as he studies me. *I know his face*, I realize. I can't think from where, but an overwhelming sense of familiarity hits me as we look at each other. He reaches forward, shaking my hand. I hadn't even realized I'd raised mine.

"Luke," he says again.

"Georgia Sayers," I reply.

We drop our hands, but his eyes keep moving over my face.

"Have we met before?" he asks, voicing my own thoughts.

"I feel like we have," I say slowly.

"Luke and I were just talking about how we went to Mooney Middle School together," Alison says, clawing her way back into the conversation. "Maybe you went there with us, Georgia."

Clever minx, already referring to the two of them like they are together. The bell rings for first period. The spell shatters. Luke and I look in opposite directions, and Taylor seizes my arm.

"Well, nice to meet you, Luke," she says. She flashes a shark-like grin at Alison. "See you, Alligator. She looks just like one, doesn't she, Luke?"

Alison's trying so hard to keep her smile on that I swear I see her eye twitch.

"Bye," I manage to say to Luke as Taylor herds me down the hall.

"Bye," he says, his words almost lost.

Taylor uses me like a battering ram as we head to our homeroom, shoving me through cracks in the crowd.

"Sparks, much?" she says under her breath as I open the door to our classroom.

I blink, still in a funk. "What?"

"That Luke guy was totally throwing you lines. 'Don't I know you?' I think that's how my Dad picked up my Mom."

We slip into our seats on the side of the room.

"No, he was right. We definitely know each other from somewhere," I say, desperately racking my brain. Still nothing comes up.

Taylor takes out her books, dropping them on the desk.

"Why did you say your last name was Sayers?" she asks, looking at me sideways.

I smack my forehead. "I did, didn't I? I don't know why I did that. It's my mother's maiden name."

"He got you all flustered, hmm?" Taylor walks her index and middle finger up my arm like a pair of tiny legs. "Ruffled your feathers a bit, *hmm*?"

I brush her off just as our teacher comes in. I bend my head to my book, but can't stop replaying the encounter in my head for the rest of the period.

The day goes by uneventfully, besides the added number of students. In some of my classes, the dislocated relief kids have to sit on the floor. I don't see Luke again, which makes me wonder if maybe he's a senior. I could have found out easily enough at our lunch period, which is juniors and seniors only, but I have to report to the library in case anyone comes by for English tutoring. Not like it's a hopping pastime on most days. It makes for a good hideout though. One encounter with Luke left me feeling like I'd misplaced my brain. I didn't want a second helping.

"Want to go for a run?" Callie asks me on the ride home. I make a face, glancing up at the clouds above us. They look bruised, angry even.

"It might rain," I argue.

"It won't. Those are stratocumulus clouds, not nimbostratus." Callie twists in her seat to see her twin. "Char, how about you?"

Charlotte rolls her eyes. "No thanks."

I get a sudden image of Charlotte running in the rain, in her dark clothes, mascara and eyeliner draining down her face. Running really wouldn't be her thing.

We pull up to the house just as my stepdad and my little sister, Abby, are getting out of the other car. His weathered, tan face brightens as he sees us. He's still in his scrubs, straight from the hospital.

"Hey girls," he says as we get out. "Where's Wyatt?"

"Football practice. He's bussing it home," I answer, walking over to hug him. As soon as I turn, Abby rushes me, thrusting a heavy plastic bag into my hands. I almost drop the giant bottles of Mane N' Tail.

"Georgia! Can you please, please make up some of Mom's shampoo for me? I'm almost out," she begs.

"Oh yeah, me too," Callie seconds as she walks past.

I groan. Abby widens her green eyes, the same eyes we all inherited, clasping her hands.

"Please, Gee. I'll make dinner tonight. You're the only one who does it right."

I'm clearly not going to win this. "Yeah, okay."

Abby jumps twice, her blonde hair swinging around her neck.

"Hey," Callie says, poking her head out the door. "Run in twenty. Be ready."

The Circle

Of course it starts raining on us halfway through the run. It's only a light sprinkle, but it's enough to make it uncomfortable. We take off jogging up the dirt trail along the road, my T-shirt sticking to me in all the wrong places. Our portly black Lab, Prince, weaves between us, lassoing my ankles with his leash. Every time he takes a step, his barrel of a belly swings into my calf. I knee him over to my other side, getting a smear of drool for my trouble.

Fat droplets of water spatter in the dirt. Callie holds up her arm to shield her eyes. "This sucks."

"I *told* you it was going to rain, but you just spouted your useless cloud knowledge at me," I say.

Callie glances at the thick belt of trees to our right.

"I bet we can find a short cut," she says. "We can hop off the trail and head through there."

Generally, we run in a big circle from our house, taking this trail that loops around a patch of forest dividing neighborhoods. I've always imagined creepy homeless guys hanging out in woods like this, waiting to prey on younglings wandering through. The drumming raindrops on my head convince me I'm being irrational. Plus, we have Prince. He's got about sixty pounds on any rapist. More teeth too.

"Okay," I concede. "But let's just go straight through. And Prince should go first."

We step over the curb, tramping into the trees. Callie unwinds the leash from her hand, letting Prince run ahead of us a little. Going "straight" is harder than I thought it would be. With no trail to follow, we're at the mercy of the trees, weaving all over the place. Luckily the wood isn't that large anymore. When we'd first moved in with my stepdad, we'd been surrounded by thick cedar forest on all sides. But over the last seven years, neighborhoods had cut it down to just this remaining island. Not that that was comforting fifty feet in, when nothing but trunks were visible.

"I gotta walk," I wheeze, slowing as a stitch wedges between my ribs.

Callie drops down to a walk too, reining in Prince. We stroll for a while, Callie kicking her legs out to stretch them. Something ahead steals her attention. She squints, pausing.

"Look at that," she says, curving off to our left. I grudgingly follow.

A few feet away, the trees fan out, creating a little clearing. Callie is standing at the center, looking down at a ring of white dust on the ground.

"It looks like a little party spot, or something," she says.

"That was definitely a fire," I say, pointing to the pile of damp ashes she's nudging with her tennis shoe.

The rain, uninhibited by the canopy, leaves pockmarks in the powdery fire pit. I walk around it, noticing the divots spaced evenly in a ring around the center. Like people had been sitting here often. I step down into one, moving closer to the moldy remains of the last fire.

The next second, it's like I've been stabbed in the stomach. White-hot agony rips my gut apart, inching deeper and deeper inside me. I double over, stumbling to my knees. I can hear Callie saying something, but I can't even open my mouth. I just sit, jaw clenched, trying to breathe through it. Wetness from the ground seeps into my skin, so cold it almost burns. I lift my hand, which has been wrist deep in mud. It comes up red. Dark blood coats my palm, dripping lazily down to my elbow. I rocket back up to my feet, despite the throbbing in my stomach. All down my shins, from knee to ankle, is drenched in crimson. More blood than could possibly be there by accident.

I frantically try to clean my legs, smearing them off with my hands. It only spreads the mess. My lungs won't function properly. Between the panic and the relentless pain, they're refusing to hold the breath I need.

"Georgia!" Callie seizes my wrists, forcing me to focus on her face.

"Please get it off me, just get it off!" I beg her.

"What are you talking about? This is mud." She waves my own hand in front of my eyes, raising her eyebrows so I get the point. "It's just mud. Calm down."

I stare at my palm. Raindrops are making quick work of clearing away the brown from my skin. Brown, not red. I look down at my legs. There's no blood.

The stabbing in my stomach ebbs, less intense with each throb, until the only thing I feel is the strong urge to throw up.

"I need to get out of here." I pull my hands away from Callie, sprinting out of the clearing. My legs seem to know where we're going. I can't focus on anything but getting out of these trees, out from under the pressure they're creating.

It's a good twenty feet before I emerge into the sweet, fresh air. I manage to gulp one breath before I face-plant into the ground. Apparently, I've come out right on the precipice of a hill. I slide a few feet down the slope, before I come to rest. Slowly, I raise myself onto my hands, spitting dirt out of my mouth. Callie appears behind me, taking the slope more carefully than I had.

"Oh my God, Gee! Are you okay?"

I sit back on my knees, examining myself. My entire front is soaked in mud, but I'm intact. It's my mind I'm worried about. My heart's still hammering behind my ears, trying to tell me something isn't right. I count the beats, just like my child therapist taught me.

I had seen blood. What piece of my brain was *still* sick enough to do that to me?

Callie seems to be stifling a laugh.

"You totally just ate it," she giggles.

"It's not funny," I grunt, standing up. "How gross do I look, on a scale of one to ten?"

"Eight and a half, but you can shower when we get home." She points down the hill. "There's the road."

From this height, we have a good view of Cody I haven't seen before. The plains are laid out right up to the hill country, sprinkled with clumps of neighborhoods. A red brick house one street over draws my eye. The white window frames tug at my memory. I realize its significance with a sinking feeling.

"What's up?" Callie asks, pinpointing my mood with that annoying ability she has.

"That's where our old house was," I say. "Where we lived before…"

I can't make myself produce more words, can't say "Before Mom died," but Callie knows. Her face closes down.

"The one that burned down?" she says stiffly.

I nod. She purses her lips, starting off down the hill. She doesn't like talking about our mother, or even being reminded we had one. I follow her after one more look at the bare yard.

We pick up our jog again when we reach the road. Every time a car sails by, I push up behind Callie, trying to hide my mottled T-shirt. She shoves me the third time I trip her.

"Stop running so close to me, Georgia," she huffs.

I open my mouth to shoot something back, but stop. Humming up the road is an old model Honda chopper, the kind my Dad would love. Straddling it is the guy from the hall, his black hair pushed back by the wind. Perfect timing. I seize Callie, making her yelp.

"Ouch, Georgia—"

"Shh, you have to hide me!"

She looks over her shoulder wildly. "Why?"

"I met that guy this morning. He *cannot* see me looking like I just crawled out of a swamp."

"What, you want me to just stand in front of you?"

"Just don't move."

She scoffs, but complies. The motorcycle growls past us, coughing occasionally. When the sound seems far enough around the bend, I break away and start jogging again.

"I hate to tell you," Callie says, catching me up. "But I'm fairly sure he could see you. Who is he, anyway?"

"Someone from Sagestone. Taylor thought he was cute," I say, brushing it off.

"Obviously she's not the only one."

I give her a cutting look, and we finish the run in silence.

I can't seem to get the shower hot enough to scald away the tingling on my legs. My skin seems to squirm under the water, refusing to shuck off the feeling that there's something on it that doesn't belong. I touch my stomach where the phantom pain had been.

When my whole body is thoroughly pink from the steam, I get out and shrug on my baggiest sweatshirt. The whole family collects at the dining room table as Abby assembles fish tacos, depositing them on plates and sliding them across the gnarled wood. Wyatt trudges in through the front door, still in uniform, shedding bags all the way to the table.

"Hey, Dad," he says, sliding in the seat next to him.

My dad already changed into his favorite T-shirt, the one that says, "I Delivered Life, What Did You Do Today?" When he squeezes Wyatt's shoulder, his laugh lines deepen as he smiles. "Good practice, kiddo?"

Wyatt shovels half a taco into his mouth. "Yep," he grunts.

Dad pans his dark brown eyes around the table. "Girls, how was your first day? Did the relief kids settle in?"

Char, Callie and I mumble our agreement.

"Did anyone talk about the Sagestone fire?"

"It was a tragedy, Dad. I'm sure they don't really want to talk about it," Callie says.

"I just don't understand how the police didn't raise a finger with all that cult stuff going on at that school. I don't want you guys to get involved with it."

"There was no cult, Dad!" Charlotte says. "The one kid that died in the fire happened to be into Wicca or something. You're way overprotective."

"Did you make my shampoo yet, Georgia?" Abby graciously interrupts, picking at the ends of her hair.

I scoop up my empty plate, heading into the kitchen. "I'll do it now."

Abby's set out the four shampoo bottles on the counter, along with the small wicker basket where Mom kept her ingredients.

She always made us this home remedy shampoo. I'd tried others, even the really expensive brands, but nothing worked like this stuff did. Our hair grew at a superhuman rate. We girls just wore it long, it was easier that way. Dad called it the "Parks' family trademark."

Parks, not Sayers, I remind myself. Parks had been my last name since I was five. Why did it feel so wrong to say it now?

My fingers open the box slowly, reveling in the tiny connection it gives me to Mom. How many times did she touch this exact box? Her fingerprints are still on the tiny glass vials inside. I make sure not to smudge them as I take a pinch from three crushed herb jars, adding it to each shampoo bottle. A few drops of select oils follow. I cap all the bottles and shake them, mixing the ingredients. Finally, I pick up the stiff post-it note tucked between the vials. Seeing her handwriting fills my chest with lead. The day she'd taught me how to do this, she'd just scribbled down the recipe and left this note, which I was supposed to read when everything was done. I thought it was cheesy at first, but now it's my favorite part of making the shampoos. I can almost hear my mother's voice as I read it out loud.

Kate St. Clair

"Long locks will grow strong, not break, or split, or wither.

Beauty within shall grow without. Remember always The Giver."

I slip the note back into the basket. I don't know what the words mean. At one point, I thought she was referencing the book, *The Giver*, since I had been reading it when I was ten and she wrote the note. Now, I think they're more for her, the woman who had given us everything. She wanted us to remember her every time we did something simple, even washing our hair.

The lid comes down with the softest click. I run my fingernail along the engraving right under the lock. *Sayers*.

Maybe it wasn't the worst thing to keep the name alive, even if I was the only one.

The Message

The Tutoring Center actually has customers by week two. Wellsey High is apparently a little more rigorous than Sagestone had been. Most of the kids who come in are people I haven't met before. With no tests on the horizon, not many people ask for an English tutor. Kids generally only come to me when they have essay tests, or to try to bribe me to write their papers. I set up camp at a corner table, trying not to feel like the rejected book nerd as I eat my lunch alone. I'm just starting my Chem worksheet when Mrs. Hall, the proctor, taps my papers.

"Georgia, you have someone," she says.

"No way!" I burst excitedly, looking up.

Luke is standing next to her, an amused look on his face. I realize my mouth is open and clap it shut.

"This is Luke," Mrs. Hall goes on, gesturing to him. "He's having trouble with senior English."

"Right," I croak, then clear my throat. "Um, why don't you sit down?"

Mrs. Hall moves away, and Luke pulls out the chair next to me.

"Georgia, right?" he asks.

"Yeah," I reply, trying to sound like I don't know *exactly* who he is. "We met the other day."

"I saw you on Skyline Loop last week," he says. "You were with someone else."

Crap. So he *had* seen me running.

"Yeah, that was my sister." I try to laugh breezily. "We were just jogging."

"It was storming," he points out. "Kind of dangerous, don't you think?"

"Says the guy riding a motorcycle without a helmet," I retort, then instantly wish I could take it back. Who was I, his mother?

Luke half-smiles, admonished. "It's my uncle's, he lets me ride it. I was bringing it home from the shop."

He glances at the homework I've been doing. A tiny "v" forms between his brows as he runs a finger over the line where I'd scribbled my name. A twinge of uneasiness pulls at my diaphragm.

"My last name is Parks," I say stupidly. "Sayers was my mother's maiden name. I seem to keep saying it lately."

He meets my eyes, and the ethereal blue of his stuns me all over again. They almost don't look human.

"I was looking at 'Georgia.' Very southern."

"Actually, it's very British. My mother was from England. My siblings are named Carolina, Charlotte, Abigail and Wyatt." I leave out Oliver James Wyatt Barnabus, just in case any of my brother's classmates are around.

He gives an impressed nod. "Sounds like an English novel."

"Speaking of novel names," I say. "What about Caulfield? Is that your real name?"

He stares at me blankly.

"Holden Caulfield? *Catcher in the Rye*?" I prompt.

Luke dips his head, his lips pulling into a smile again. "I guess that's why I'm here. I'm having a lot of trouble getting what we're doing in English, and I'm not really used to reading in—" he stops randomly, blinking, as if he'd said something he hadn't meant to.

After a second, I cut in. "Well, I can definitely help you. I love English, it's kind of my thing."

Luke reaches into his backpack, setting his notebook on the table. He seems so out of place here in the library. He should be somewhere outside, maybe hiking or rafting, not bent over notes. He hands one of his books to me. "This is what we're working on."

"*The Aeneid*! Such a classic." I sigh.

He gives me that bemused look again, like I'd said something unexpected.

"I can tell you everything you need to know about this book," I promise.

Luke spreads his hands. "Let's do it."

Luke is the perfect listener. Usually, people I tutor argue with me, or insist I'm making stuff up. They get frustrated and stop paying attention. Luke stays with me the whole time, locked on my face. He even takes notes! No one has ever thought my ideas were important enough the write down.

When lunch is over, Mrs. Hall circles the tables, reminding us all. Regretfully, I stand up, sweeping my books into my bag. Luke shoulders his backpack, looking down at me.

"This was surprisingly fun. When do you tutor, usually? Just Wednesdays?" he asks.

I stare at him in shock. No one's ever come back for a repeat session.

"I'm here Monday, Wednesday, Friday at lunch, so you can kind of pick what day."

"Friday then." He flashes me a disarming smile. "Can't wait."

Luke strides past me. I stay rooted to the spot, trying to decide if I'd actually heard right. I shake my head, smiling at my naïveté. He's just being nice to me, the nerdy tutor girl. Guys like him date girls like Alison. Or they try to date Taylor, but get shot down. Someone like me isn't even on his radar.

I stalk out of the library, twisting the strap of my bag and trying not to let disappointment get the best of me. I'd be stronger next time. Next time, I wouldn't play into his hands so easily.

A few people are clumped around my locker wing, making a very inconvenient barrier. I try to skirt around them politely, then realize no one is talking. The girl closest to me meets my eye, and I can almost see her retreating away from me in her mind. Like smoke dissolving into the air, the group disperses in opposite directions. When I step up to my locker, my bag slips out of my hands. All six of my books land on top of my foot, but I barely even flinch.

The tattered wing of a bird has been nailed into my locker door.

It hangs there lifelessly, the pale grey feathers contrasting with the yellow paint behind them. It's small enough to be a dove's, or maybe a pigeon's.

Under the gift, someone wrote a message in streaked, red letters...

WE SEE YOU.

Gemma Sayers

The nail doesn't come out easily. Whoever left me the heartwarming message meant it to stick. I carry a shifting queasiness in my stomach for the rest of class. Every scrape of my pen against paper reminds me of the pierced sinew of the tissuey wing.

The twins had signed up for track and Anime Club respectively, and with Wyatt at football, I had the car to myself for two hours. The thought of returning to our empty, isolated house seems unbearable, so I decide to go see Gemmie.

The road out to her house had given up on its job of creating safe transport years ago, and my SUV was meant more for puttering at twenty miles an hour than off-roading. It's always worth it, though, to finally turn off and see her little stone cottage. My last living grandparent hadn't brought anything when she came from England, but someone managed to erect a page from *British Homes* smack in the

Texas countryside. The cottage sits like an enchanted picture, an oasis between rough pecan trees, all stone and windows.

I park and hop down from my car. Ducking under some wayward vine tendrils, I reach to knock on the door, but it swings open before I make contact. Gemmie's elegant face pokes through the doorframe, breaking into a smile when she sees me.

"Darling," she says, her crisp accent ringing. "Come in, I made tea."

Gemmie lets me in, herding me into her tiny kitchen. I sit at her tiny round table in the breakfast nook, watching her sweep around the stove, the billowy blue cloth of her dress trailing in her wake. When I was little, I was convinced she was Titania, queen of the faeries. Sometimes I still get glimpses of it. In the way her feet never seem to shuffle, how she swirls the air around her as she plucks the kettle off the stove.

Her fat Siamese cat lands heavily on my thigh before heaving himself up my arm to sit backward on my shoulder. His flab hangs over either side of my shoulder, and a thunderous purr vibrates my throat. Gemmie returns, setting my tea in front of me.

"How are you, my heart?" She says as she sits in the chair opposite me.

From the nose up, she still reminds me so much of my mother. Were it not for the silver-grey braid and fine lines that touched her eyes and mouth, she could have been Mom's sister. They had the same strong brow, and the same way of keeping it completely motionless when they know something is wrong. I don't see the point in hedging, so I say, "Some kid left this on my locker. And I'm seeing things again."

I set the detached wing on the table. Even through four layers of paper towels, I feel like I'm touching the lifeless feathers.

Gemmie gingerly opens the bundle, one layer at a time. "What did you see?"

"Just a lot of blood. We were in the woods behind our neighborhood."

The last layer comes up, and her fingers pause.

"Poor little thing," she says after a moment.

"I thought maybe we could bury it?" I say. It sounds so juvenile, but it feels like the right thing to do.

Gemmie swiftly refolds the bundle. "Yes, I think that's a very good idea."

"I don't understand why people are still doing this to us. I thought it was over."

The real weight of my disappointment settles on top of me like cement. It'd been so long since the spray painting, the whispered insults, the hate that followed the fire. Back then, people hadn't looked at us. Kids weren't allowed to be friends with us. Superstition clung to my family like leprosy, something scarring that everyone could see. I thought we'd finally managed to crawl out from under the Parks' legacy, but this was in a class all its own.

"Georgia," Gemmie says, gathering my hand in both of hers. "This is not about you. It's about fear. Always has been. That is the only power anyone can have over you. You have to be stronger than your fear."

An hour later, when she's stuffed me with half a loaf of walnut-studded tea bread and the warmth has returned to my stomach, I head back out to my car. At the door, Gemmie wraps me in her thin frame.

"Don't let it weigh on you, my pet," she says.

I nod as we break apart.

"And here," she adds, bending to a stringy shrub to the right of the door. She breaks off one of the tendrils and threads it through the strap of my backpack, typing in into a knot. Amazingly, it doesn't break, just hangs there in a ratty ring. "My grandmother used to give me a string of this whenever I needed some extra luck. Maybe it'll help."

"Thanks, Gemmie. Love you," I say, waving as I turn toward the driveway.

As soon as I'm perched in the driver's seat, I pull the plant stem off. It's exactly the kind of thing I shouldn't show up to school with. Something that looked weird and unexplainable. As I reverse out, I see Gemmie slip out the back door into her garden. She's got the wadded paper towels cradled in her elbow.

Tattoo

"Georgia!"

I spot Taylor's frantically waving arm rising above the mass of students in the cafeteria. I hold my tray over my head and wade through the undulating throng. Lunch has turned into a music festival situation, with some kids forced to sit on each other's laps.

I wedge in next to our friend Gallagher, who's eating from four different bags of chips.

"What up, Gee?" He flashes me his oversized grin with just a tad too much gum.

"Hey, Gally," I reply.

Taylor turns to the pale girl with a blazing red ponytail that's settled next to her.

"Georgia, this is M.C., of the late Sagestone High School," she says, making a grandiose gesture to the girl. M.C. offers me a wave.

"Nice to meet you," I say. "M.C., what's that stand for?"

"Marie-Claire," she answers, pulling a face. "My mom didn't realize she was naming me after the stupidest magazine in the world."

I laugh, liking her already.

"The Alison-beast is on the prowl," Taylor says, glaring over my shoulder.

When I twist around, Alison's sheet of plasticky blonde hair catches my eye from across the room like light on a mirror. She's turned sideways at her table, rambling into Luke's ear. She's practically on his lap.

M.C. groans, tilting her head back. "Ugh, Luke Caulfield is so hot. He's got that 'I love you but I might kill you' thing going on."

Gallagher chokes out a Dorito-powdered laugh. "That's what the girls like these days? Impending death by strangling?"

"Everyone at Sagestone thought he was a creep," M.C. goes on, taking a swipe at Gallagher. "Probably still would, but the fire actually did him some favors. Everyone wants to know if he did it. Something about having an arsonist in your circle seems to entice people."

"Why would they think he did it?" I break in.

"Because he was the only person who talked to Matthew Townsend, the kid who died. *That guy* was a creeper to the fifth degree. He was a Satanist or something, and Luke was into it, too, apparently. They hung out like every day up until the fire. The police said it was just a prank gone wrong, but I would bet a hundred bucks Matthew set the fire as like a sacrifice to the Devil, and lost his soul in the process." She finishes with a raspy, ominous tone, meant to sway our opinion.

"In this circle, we don't judge the religious inclinations of others," Taylor asserts heavy handedly, raising her eyes at me. She was probably the only person who relished my mother's stigma.

"Thanks for that," I say flatly.

My mood has just taken a nosedive. If what M.C. said was true, Luke had lost a friend in the fire. I knew all to well what it felt like to lose people for no reason, have them just vanish out from under you, leave you falling. I didn't have to know him to know the aching emptiness that hung inside him, followed him everywhere. We had something in common, at least.

When school lets out, I squeeze myself into a stall in the locker room to change. My days of running near my house are dead and gone. I've resigned to run along the track in full view of many, many people.

As I pull out the shorts I packed, I groan. I'd accidentally grabbed Callie's tiny Soffee shorts instead of my longer ones. They look great on Callie, who is seventy percent leg, but they are a little daring for me.

Halfway down to the track, there's a wolfish whistle from behind me. I wheel around and spot Taylor walking with M.C. and Gallagher toward the parking lot.

"Work those tiny shorts, Gee," Taylor jeers, winding her arm like she was about to make a softball pitch.

I yank the shorts down as best I can. "They're Callie's," I yell back at her.

She makes some whooping noises, drawing everyone's attention within twenty feet.

"I hate you," I shout, half-jokingly.

She blows a kiss at me. I turn around and manage to stop myself right before I collide with Luke's back. He's leaning on the fence that borders the track, looking out at the sprinters preparing for warm up. He spots me, a confused look taking over his face.

"Oh, hey," he says. "I thought that was you out there."

He gestures to the other side of the track, where Callie is stretching with her back to us. She does look slightly like me from behind, I notice. If I were the type to wear blindingly pink jogging shorts.

"Ah, stalking me, are you?" I say.

Luke laughs softly. It's a strange laugh, without any sound. Just a grin accompanied by a breath out.

"Thanks for calling me out," he says.

Alison, clad in spandex and not much else, stares at me from amidst the mass of cross country runners, looking like she wants to set me on fire. So that's who Luke was really watching.

"Are you thinking of joining track?" I ask, holding Alison's stare until she turns around and bends over, presumably stretching her hamstrings.

"No, just on my way to the pool," Luke answers. "I was on the swim team at Sagestone. I'm hoping they'll let me jump on here."

I blow out a low whistle. "I could never do that. The thought of swimming in the winter makes me want to cry."

Luke shrugs. "Never bothered me. I'm a water guy."

He rakes his fingers along his scalp, and as his hand falls back down, I notice a blotch of color on his forearm. The sleeve of his jacket is bunched up in the crook of his elbow, and a half circle of red ink is poking out.

"Is that a tattoo?" I blurt.

His smile disappears like it's been whisked away by a fishing line. He tugs his sleeve down to the wrist.

"Yes."

"Is it a pentagram?" I'm mildly impressed at my power of recall.

He swallows, shifting to his left foot, away from me. "Sort of. My parents practiced this certain tradition of Wicca, it has to do with that. But I'm not like…completely into it."

"Hey, no judgment," I say weakly.

His gaze flicks back to me, almost guiltily. "I've freaked you out."

"No, no. If anyone understands weird parents, it's me," I say, glancing in Alison's direction. "A lot of people don't like my family just because of some stupid rumors about my mother."

Luke tilts his head. "What rumors?"

I hit a mental block, the wall my brain always throws up when I start talking about Mom. But something in me needs to tell him, if only to keep Alison from poisoning one more person against me.

"My mother made herbal remedies, like holistic medicines and stuff, and for a while she worked as a midwife with my dad. She was really good, but she lost one baby, and then everyone said she was a witch who killed children."

I blink. Had that all really just come out of my mouth? I had known this guy two weeks, and I'm already spilling family secrets.

Luke presses his lips together. "Hmm. It's interesting hearing your side of it."

So he's heard already.

He shoulders his duffle bag, offering me a slight wave. "See you around."

As he heads down toward the lap pool, I give myself an internal slap on the hand. I shouldn't be digging up stories about my mother, especially with someone already trying to stir something up. I step onto the track and set off at a jog, counterclockwise to what the track team is doing. As I near the group, Callie gives me an up and down scan.

"I want my shorts back," she hisses when she's in earshot.

"Gladly. And maybe tomorrow you can buy some that aren't from Babies 'R' Us," I shoot back.

Oggun

After dinner, I creep into my dad's office to set up my laptop. It was one of the few places our ancient house allowed WiFi to pass through with anything close to speed. My fingers type "Wicca" into the search browser seemingly without my direction. Eleven million results answer my query. Most are trying to sell me "Authentic Sacrificial Daggers," but a few offer histories or guidelines. There are too many sects to even count, it seems.

Some have the sinister, threatening feel that had given witchcraft such a bad rap, but others seemed… benign. Most of what I find is for healing with herbs, or spells to gain courage, or change your luck. No more freaky than any other religion. As I flick through the websites, I wonder which one Luke is involved with.

"What are you looking at?" Callie's voice says over my shoulder. My stomach takes a flying leap into my ribcage.

"Jeez, Cal," I say, blowing out a breath.

She leans forward, studying the screen. Her eyes slide to me. "Okay, freak."

I roll the chair closer to the desk, blocking her out.

"There's a kid at my school who's Wiccan or something. I was just curious," I say.

She arches an eyebrow at me, popping a piece of chocolate in her mouth. "You really think you should be digging this stuff up? With that display someone left on your locker? You're just giving people a reason to hate you."

"It's my life, thanks," I say.

She shrugs, padding out of the study. I tap my finger on the track pad, thinking, then search: "metaphysical, Cody TX." One address in Austin comes up, so I quickly scribble it down.

"Cat bomb!"

I whirl in the chair just in time to see Wyatt toss Ruby, our grey and white cat, at me. She's not happy, and she lands on my legs with all twenty claws out.

I let out a sound like "*gyah!*"

"Wyatt, you stupid idiot!" I shout, prying Ruby off my jeans.

He laughs hysterically, running back into the hall. I set Ruby on the ground and peel the post-it off the stack. Tomorrow is Saturday; I'd have a chance to explore a little.

Austin is only about half an hour from Cody, but the expanse of flatlands in between makes you feel like you're making a trek across the desert. Every time I get to come into town, it's a bit like rounding the corner to see The Emerald City clustered in front of you. There are actual businesses and buildings higher than one story, and the dusty brown quality of Cody's streets doesn't seem to hold sway here.

The address I had was on the numbered streets downtown, east of the highway. When I get close enough, I ease off I-35 onto the frontage road. When I stop at a light, I have the briefest twinge of second thoughts. My dad wasn't strict, we had few rules—we called it "stepdad syndrome"—but the one thing he insisted on was never venturing east of the highway. That rule was meant for nighttime excursions, but part of me knew he wouldn't be happy if he found out what I was doing. But then, the whole purpose of the trip would probably make him rethink my car privileges. I was in this now, better to go for broke.

When I start to think I've gone too deep into the warehouse district, I see it. It isn't the earthy, hippie-infused hutch I thought it would be. It's one in a line of brick squares, set apart only by the sprawling murals painted across the front. The symbol of a huge bird takes up most of the wall, its wings stretching from one side to the other. Its claws clutch a scythe.

Oggun, the store name, is spray painted over the doors like a black halo.

I park a few blocks down, noting I'm the only car on the street. *It is Texas*, I reassure myself. Even in Austin, which was by far the most open city in the state, there would never be a line out the door for a place like this.

I'm about to go in when writing on right side of the wall draws my eye. Someone's done this by hand, not a spray can. It reads, *"Muerte Se Lleve Ninguno De Nosotros."* I try to piece a meaning together. Death, something. Death carries no one? That can't be right.

I pull open the door. For such a large building, the shop is surprisingly small. The back wall seems to be a construct, a thick wall of curtains from ceiling to floor that halves the room. Rows and rows of aged wooden shelves rib the center, all laden with baskets and jars. I wander to the nearest shelf, leaning down to peer at twine-wrapped bundles of dried leaves. A hand written sign in front of the wicker basket labels them "white sage."

I'd been to a place like this before, but it hadn't been nearly as well stocked. My mother had brought us to a *curandera* a few times, a healer. Someone who used herbs to make medicines, just like she did. But the woman she went to lived in a tiny shack out in the country, and her stock was stuffed into clay pots. Nothing on this scale.

A man ducks out from between the curtains, moving lazily like the customer waits for him. He fights the strong urge to roll his eyes when he sees me.

"Just curious?" he asks. I can't help feeling a bit sorry for the guy. He probably deals with ten people a day wandering through just to get a thrill of doing something edgy. I have the strong urge to prove to him how sincere I am.

"I'd actually really like any information you can give me. Do you have any books?"

He's such a gangly thing, maybe just out of college. When he moves to the checkout counter, he looks almost like a grasshopper that just found out it can walk on two legs. He produces a clipboard, smudging his fist across his forehead wearily as he holds it out to me.

"We offer subscriptions to *Witches Monthly*. That's the best I got."

I take the clipboard and outstretched pen defiantly. "Perfect. I just put my name and address?"

"We only take cash," he adds. With his country accent, it takes him a painfully long time to get the four words out.

"That's fine," I say, writing my name across the top line.

I'm halfway through my street name when he says, "Pay first."

"Okay." I try not to get irked, just set the clipboard on the counter and fish out my wallet. I want to punch myself when I see only nine dollars in the pocket.

"Sorry, how much is it?" I ask, looking up. The guy is locked onto the subscription form, his eyes refusing to blink. When he snaps his head back to me, his face has changed. His jaw is clenched, and his irises bob in the whites of his eyes like pool floats. I take a step back.

"This is your name?" he asks. I glance briefly at it, realizing I made the mistake of writing Sayers instead of Parks again. Annoying misstep, but it didn't deserve the twitchy reaction I was getting.

"Yeah. But listen, I don't have enough cash right now. I'm going to have to come back."

"No," he says quickly. "It's free. Just... can you wait here for a second?"

His upper lip is getting slick. My stomach retracts, and I hitch at the uncomfortable pressure that wells up inside me. It's like someone has a hand around my diaphragm and is squeezing, squeezing.

"I need to go now," I rasp, fighting down a drift of nausea.

Fingers grip my forearm, like snakes wrapping around prey. The guy looks just as surprised as me by his action, but doesn't loosen the hold.

"Let me go," I say, remarkably evenly.

"Just stay for a second," he says desperately.

I pull myself backward, dragging him along for the first few steps until he gets his feet under him.

"Let go!" I yell, twisting my arm to pry his fingers off.

He swings me to the left, knocking me into one of the shelves. When I trip, I take him with me. We both sprawl out on the floor, dried herbs raining down on us. His elbow digs into my thigh as he works for a better hold, and I keep shoving him off with my knees. His hand makes it to the back of my neck, index finger digging into the base of my skull. Words start pouring out of his mouth, hushed and hurried, and heat starts to blossom under his fingertip. His left arm is right in front of my mouth, so I take my only option and bite down on it as hard as I can. He lets out a catlike yowl, and all the pressure disappears.

I throw myself onto my feet, sprinting out of the store. My knees feel every slam of my feet against pavement as I run up the street, internally kicking myself for parking so far away.

When I finally reach the SUV, I throw my bag on the hood to dig for my keys. It doesn't look like he's following, but I need to be as far away from this place as possible. Movement to my left makes me jump a foot, a short yelp tearing from my mouth.

A very small Mexican woman puts a warm hand on my shoulder. Despite the hammering in my ears, I manage to not burst into tears at the sight of her.

"This man just attacked me, can you call the police?" I say. She shakes her grey-streaked head, the lines in her forehead folding over each other.

"*La lechuza*," she says. Her dark eyes search my face for confirmation.

"Lo siento, no hablo bien Español," I ramble in my badly halting version of Spanish. *"Neccesito ayuda."*

Her other hand catches my right arm. *"La lechuza te esta buscando."*

I open my door, backing away from her. *"No comprende, los siento."*

This was the culmination of my three years of Spanish class, not even being able to tell a woman to call the police. I pull the SUV back, skirting around her. She stares after me, those black eyes never leaving my face.

Gypsy

There's a storm over Cody as I drive home, thunderheads pushing out of the mass like cobras. The woman on the police line I talk to seems less than impressed by my complaint, and suggests that if I want to avoid that kind of situation I shouldn't go to "those places." She doesn't even promise a follow-up.

I throw my phone down hard into the cup holder, irritation rattling around in my stomach like coins in a can. My fingers go to the back of my neck. The nerves in the little bowl of my skull feel raw and tender. In fact none of me feels quite right. Every shadow across the passenger seat makes my heart seize, preparing to launch me into survival mode. When the post-it note flutters in the AC, I almost slam into the bumper of the car in front of me, I twitch so badly.

I pull off the road at the next cluster of buildings. I'm in south Cody, where the town square is, but from there home seems hours away. I can't trust myself to drive even that far, with the way my hands are twitching every time I see movement. If I can just sit, just get my head around it, my body will catch up. I pull into a parking lot tucked between two cafés, both too polished to have been in town long. Gypsy, the building to the left, I've actually heard of from Taylor. They serve entirely organic food, farmed locally. That was more of an Austin fad, but even Cody wasn't immune to the influence. The sapphire blue walls of the exterior alone make it look like a gemstone tossed in the washed out, sun-leached scenery of Cody.

I get out. I'm not hungry, completely the opposite, but a cup of tea sounds like it could save my life. Even at such an awkward time of day, patrons are still filtering around the patio. I pull open the doors, cold air brushing across my cheeks. I pick a two-person booth, nestle against the wall, and tuck my feet under me. It feels slightly better to be around people. I look around the café, awed by the artistry of it. Every inch of the walls is painted by hand, scenes of dancing gypsies and white birds, caravans and palm readers.

"Georgia?"

My feet come down, ready to propel myself out of the booth. Luke is standing on the other side of my table.

"Who's stalking who now?" He smiles, those aquamarine eyes dancing against his skin.

"I was just on my way home," I say quickly. "Do you work here?"

There's the tiniest crack of disappointment in his face. "This is my aunt and uncle's place. I help them out when I can. You really didn't know I work here?"

I notice the Gypsy logo on his white shirt, right over his heart, and the towel tucked into his jeans. "I didn't know that."

"You okay?" That little "v" engraves itself between his eyebrows.

I take a breath, about to recount the episode at Oggun, but I catch myself. The only reason I'd gone was to learn more about him and what he did. I'd driven all the way into Austin to do it. Not the kind of thing I wanted to admit right after showing up randomly at his aunt and uncle's restaurant.

"I'm having a weird day," I finish carefully. An idea lights up behind his eyes.

"Wait right here. I got your back." He turns away, rounding the corner into the kitchen.

A moment later he returns, balancing a squat green teapot in his left hand and a plate in the other. He spreads out tea and cups and a four-inch thick slice of cinnamon-sugar cake in front of me.

"On the house. If it doesn't make you feel better, I'll bring you lunch for a week. Promise."

"You're not a very good salesman," I say, carving out a forkful of cake. It dissolves on my tongue into warm, buttery softness, trailing a comforting heat all the way down to my stomach when I swallow. I do my best not to sigh. It's exactly what I need, good old-fashioned fat and sugar.

"If you want to share, that's totally an option," Luke says, picking up his own fork and digging in.

"Is it allowed for waiters to steal from customers," I tease.

"I'm not a waiter, I'm a busboy. And I just got off." When he reaches out for another bite, I catch the trace or reddish brown at his elbow again. He's not wearing a long sleeve, but his T-shirt still covers the entirety of his biceps.

"Do you always wear long sleeves so people won't see your tattoos?" It's out of my mouth before I realize how rude a question that is.

He chews roughly, obviously uncomfortable. "Yeah. People kind of judge you if you don't."

"How does that work with the swim team? Don't they see?"

"Swim tees." He itches at his left arm, where the half-moon of pentagram rests in his elbow.

"How far up do they go?" I ask.

He swallows heavily. With his index, he points to the pentagram, then drags his finger up his arm, across his chest in a downward "v," then up to his right shoulder and down to the other elbow.

"Wow," I say. I can't picture him with those harsh red symbols scattered across his body. They seem too hard for him.

He puts both of his elbows on the table, leaning closer. "Why are you so interested in them?"

I shrug, answering honestly. "It's all interesting. I never grew up with *one* religion, but because of my mom, we never touched anything remotely witchy. Even with the scary parts, I still think it could be cool."

"There doesn't have to be scary parts," he says. "It's the people that make it scary, not the craft."

I press my mouth into a line.

"For real," he insists. "Look at my aunt and uncle. Everyone in my family grew up as *brujas*. My mom and her two sisters were from a tiny town in Mexico, and they all got taught the same thing. My mom took it to a bad place. My aunt Idra, even worse. But Iona, she took the good parts. About loving the earth, and using what it gives us to heal people. About using your energy to make good things happen. That's what it's about."

"She sounds great," I say genuinely.

His face warms. "She is. She and Finn, they're more parents to me than my mother and father ever were. I ran away when I was thirteen, they took me in. They showed me that religion shouldn't be a weapon. Which, now, I'm going to show you."

He digs a pen out of his pocket, pulling my paper napkin in front of him. His hand moves over the square quickly, filling it up with his boyish, scrawling handwriting. "I'm writing you a spell to try. Worst case, it won't do anything for you. Best case, maybe it'll give you a clear mind. Try burning a candle when you say the words."

He gives it to me, his hand hovering in the air as he says, "Actually, come with me."

Luke slips out of the booth, taking my wrist in his long fingers. I scoot out after him, letting him lead me down the aisles of tables into the back of the café. We squeeze down a hallway, Luke opening a door to the right.

The tiny room we go in shimmers like a diamond mine. All along the walls hang strands of beads and necklaces with pendants ranging from pea-sized to bigger than lemons. Against the far wall, a rugged wooden desk is barely visible beneath spools of twine and jars of whole gemstones, still rough and uncut.

Luke wanders to the left wall, scanning the dangling pendants.

"Iona makes these," he says, pausing to delicately pluck a thin silver chain off its nail. "Stones have energies, and each one is different. When you have the stone, it gives its energy to you. This one is amethyst."

He rests the chain with a tiny purple stone in twisted silver in my palm.

"It's beautiful," I say, holding it up so glows violet in the light. "So all these stones do something different?"

Luke nods, glancing around.

"Some make you open to love, or heal you, or give you strength. But this will do for now. It'll help open your mind." He takes the necklace, unfastening the hook. "Lift up your hair."

"I can't take it," I say quickly. "I'll buy it. I'd love to."

"She doesn't sell them. She gives them away."

I watch the perfect tiny orb sway from the silver chain. "It's too beautiful. Give me an ugly one."

"Shut up and take your gift," he grins.

I relinquish, gathering my hair off my neck. He leans over my shoulder to fasten it. He's so close. I can feel the warmth from his skin, smell chlorine mixed with laundry sheets in his T-shirt. He steps back to survey me, taking the warmth and leaving me chilled.

"Looks good," he says.

We walk out together, Luke waving goodbyes to every staff member he passes. Outside, wet wind sweeps through the street, buffeting us as we head toward my car.

"What are your plans for today?" Luke asks.

"I have to do chores at home," I say, touching the tiny gem where it hangs in the hollow of my throat. "What about you?"

"I think I'll go swimming in the lake before it rains," he answers with a grin. "You're welcome to join."

I look up at the clouds. They've turned gangrenous, laden with the kind of heavy heat that births ground lightning.

"No thanks. I like living," I say.

Luke laughs that quiet laugh. It's the second time I've heard it and I already know it by heart. The wind snatches my hair up, twisting it across my eyes. Before I can move it, Luke's brushed it away, letting it thread through his fingers. He seems to realize what he's doing, and drops his hand like it's made of lead.

"It's long," he says.

"Yeah. Kind of a family trait." I wrap my arms around my chest, suddenly feeling like I'm not wearing enough. My fingers brush the tender skin on my left arm where the shopkeeper's vise of a grip had landed.

"I guess I'll see you Monday for tutoring," he says. "Let me know how the incantation works."

I nod. "Yup, I'll let you know if I turn into a goat."

He snorts, turning toward the far end of the parking lot where the old chopper waits like a lopsided black horse.

"There's worse things that cute goats," he says, waving over his shoulder.

SPELLED

The Eleven-Year Spell

I have to wait until Sunday night to try the incantation, when there's a lull in the house after dinner. Everyone's retreated to their rooms, leaving the halls in a sort of suspended silence. If there's a time to try Luke's meditation, it's now. I hunt around our pantry for some unscented candles, eventually locating the dust-caked cardboard box mom had kept them in. I choose a thick white pillar candle with whorls in the creamy wax, clearly homemade.

When I've scrounged some matches, I retreat back to my room. Folding my legs under me, I set the candle on the floor. The wick takes up the flame with a tiny *pffft!* I take Luke's note out, reading it over until the words stick in my mind. Eyes closed, I take a series of deep breaths, as per Luke's instructions. The words leave my lips in a hushed stream.

"*Open my third eye,*
Open my mind's eye,
Help me to see the unseen.

Let me Be as I have never been,
Let me See as I have never seen.
Release my soul within."

At the exact moment I'm done saying it, an unseen force slams into my shoulders, pitching me backward until I smack into the floorboards. It feels like a railroad spike is being shoved between my eyes, breaking open my head as it goes. I want to scream, or throw up, but no sound comes from my mouth. I try to roll, to move my arms, but my body has been cut off. My vision is flooded with a sheet of white. The nerves behind my eyes are trembling in agony, trying to get a hold on what's happening.

Just as quickly as it came, the pain is gone. My ceiling materializes above me, as plain and grey as before. I force myself to sit up, running a check on my body. I feel... okay.

Shaky, disturbed, but physically I'm all right. I stretch my hands out in front of me, trying to feel any speck of difference.

My door drifts open, and Charlotte walks in. I scream.

Charlotte reels back against the wall, pressing her hand over her heart, wide-eyed.

"Jesus, Georgia, what?" she gasps.

"You're on fire!" I shout, jumping to my feet. I grab the blanket off my bed, remembering you're supposed to smother clothes fires.

Crackling, orange-red flames engulf Charlotte's whole body, as she spins, looking at herself. Seeming to see nothing, she raises her eyes to me.

"Is that supposed to be funny? You freaking scared the crap out of me."

I freeze, halfway through throwing my blanket at her. She can't see it. *How* can she not see it? The air around her whips with the orange tongues of it, so fierce it's a wonder the walls don't catch fire. *It's not real,* my rational mind tells me harshly. *You know it's not real.*

"No, uh," I stammer, "I just, I thought I saw it."

Charlotte narrows her eyes at me. "Okay. Well, do you want to come downstairs? We were going to have ice cream. Maybe you should be with people for a bit."

"No thanks, I feel kind of sick," I lie. Each word sounds like a kick to a piece of sheet metal as I say it. "I think I need to go to bed."

Concern crosses Charlotte's face. "You want some ginger?"

I shake my head. "Just sleep, probably."

Charlotte nods and shuts the door softly. I climb into my bed, feeling like I've run a marathon. My brain spins in circles, trying to process what I've just seen. I'm too tired to get a hold on it all. I can't even try. My head sinks into my pillow, and I'm asleep in seconds.

In my dream, I'm lying against the old wood floorboards of our house in Louisiana, my back pressed against the underside of my mom's bed. There are voices outside our room.

Then it's blackness, and I'm paralyzed, a huge weight lying across my body. I feel eyes, someone's gaze on me, sending an itch skittering across my skin. I know he's smiling. He's watching me squirm like a butterfly being pinned to paper.

"There you are," his voice says. "Georgia."

My eyes snap open. It's morning, and I'm alone. The walls of my room are brushed with watery blue light, reassuring me that the night is over. My clothes are soaked, hanging to me in clammy wrinkles. They feel like wet hands on my body as I sit up.

Ruby, our cat, is at the foot of my bed. Occasionally, she did creepy things like this, staring at us while we're sleeping. But Ruby is just sitting, eyes closed. I nudge her with my toe.

Her head cracks to the side with a muffled snap. It hangs there, bent at an angle, and her eyelids retract. Underneath are not the eyes of a living thing. They're cold and moldered, covered by a thick blue-grey film.

I shoot backward in bed. Before I can scream, she's vanished. Flicked in and out of existence in a second. *It's not real,* I tell my pulsing heart. *Be stronger than the fear.*

I head straight to the bathroom to douse my face with icy water. When I catch my reflection, my toothbrush clatters out of my hand.

"What the hell?" I say aloud, leaning forward to look at myself.

I'm surrounded by a roiling, gold-flecked cloud. It moves almost like a storm in fast forward, growing, collapsing, and growing again.

I don't even bother with a morning routine, just tug on a T-shirt and go downstairs. In the kitchen, I pull out a tub of cookie dough, digging into it with a spoon. The sugar granules and melting chocolate on my tongue make me feel mildly better.

"Eww," Callie says, coming into the kitchen for her cereal. "How can you eat that so early in the morning?"

I stare at her for a second before answering. She has a rosy, glowing circle around her that reminds me of early sunset. I dig out another spoonful.

"I'm having a bad day," I say.

Callie sips her apple juice. "All ready?"

Confrontation

It gets worse. As soon as I walk into school, the tumult begins. Colors and temperature shifts batter me, coming form a thousand different sources. I dip my head, focusing only on the floor, and power through the crowd. My only mindset is to find the person responsible for this.

I reach the senior locker wall, stopping when I see a pair of black sneakers that could only belong to Luke. I raise my eyes, but Luke's upper half is shielded by his locker door.

"Luke."

The door shuts and he turns to me. His eyes widen several centimeters.

"Whoa," he says.

That's when I know he can see it too.

"Yeah, whoa," I snap. "I can't stop seeing these things," I lower my voice to a hiss, gesturing to the cloud, "around my siblings. I feel like I'm going crazy. I just want it to stop!"

To my horror, my eyes sting, threatening tears. I fill my lungs, steeling myself. The color around Luke draws my attention, a deep, sapphire blue that ripples like water.

Luke takes my arm in his hand. "Look, let's go outside."

Fabulous idea. I stare at the ground again as Luke steers me towards the doors. We burst outside into the fresh air. I close my eyes, letting the silence surround me. Luke wheels me around to face him, bending at the waist a little so he can look directly into my eyes.

"Tell me exactly what you're seeing," he orders.

Over Luke's shoulder, a tree draws my attention. The rough brown of the trunk it turning black, as if it's burning without fire. It's dying right in front of me, caving in. The leaves drop off, and the dead tree crumbles to the ground, twisting back up into the air as dust. My mouth hangs open in shock.

"What's up, what do you see?" Luke asks, his brow creasing.

"That tree just died."

Luke glances over his shoulder, but apparently sees nothing.

"Did you see an omen?" he asks.

"What does that even mean, 'an omen?' I have no idea what I'm seeing. What did that spell do? Why didn't you tell me this would happen?" I clamp my jaw so my lip won't twitch.

Luke pulls back, holding his hands up. "Georgia, I had no clue this would happen. I'm sorry. Just sit down here for a second. I promise this'll help."

He sinks down to the grass, cross-legged. After a pause, I follow suit.

"Lean back on the ground," he commands, stripping off his jacket and handing it to me. "Use that as a pillow."

I want to comment on his bossy tone, but I'm running on fumes as it is. I slip the jacket under my head, feeling the cool grass pressing against my back. The open, blue sky extends above me, and it's a relief not to see anything weird for just a moment.

"Are you going to explain what's going on?" I ask.

Luke twists something off his index finger. He hands me a thin, silver ring with a tiny, striped orange stone set in it. I hadn't even noticed him wearing it.

"Put that on," he says. I slip the ring onto my middle finger, the only one it even remotely fits. It hangs loosely enough that I can spin it slowly.

"That's carnelian," Luke says, tapping the stone. "It focuses your mind, keeps out unwanted distractions."

Glancing up at Luke, I notice the dark blue had disappeared.

"Thank you," I say before sighing.

Luke nods.

"Just keep that on until you learn to focus your thoughts a little more. And maybe take this off." He points to the amethyst necklace at my throat.

My fingers grasp the thin chain, and I'm strangely distressed at the thought of losing it. Still, if it's going to help. I unclasp it and hand it to him.

"Okay, first of all," Luke starts, folding his hands. "That incantation I gave you isn't supposed to do that much. It's just meant to remove mental barriers, like prejudices. The only thing I can think of that happened is that you pulled too much energy. Did you do the spell exactly the way I wrote it down?"

"*Yes*," I snap defensively.

"That still wouldn't explain this," he says to himself, gesturing to where the golden cloud had surrounded me. "What you're seeing, peoples' auras and omens, those are things that only witches see."

"Okay, but I'm not a witch. I only did the one spell, and obviously I messed that up."

"That's not what I mean. There are people who practice witchcraft, and there are actual, full-blooded *witches*. People who are born to it."

I sit up on my elbow, looking at him. "So?"

"So," Luke looks at the ground. "You said people thought your mother might have been a witch, right?"

I feel fury and hurt rising up in my chest. "She wasn't."

"Look, Georgia." His fingers rest on my collarbone. "You need to consider the possibility that she was."

Before he's even finished, I bat his hand off me and wrestle to my feet, brushing the grass off my jeans in violent swats. My mind scrambles for something to grasp onto, something that makes sense. Is this some sort of elaborate prank? Could he have drugged me somehow?

"She *wasn't*," I say. "And if this is something Alison put you up to, it's not funny. Screw you both."

I turn away, not even looking at his reaction. After two steps, his hands grab my shoulders, spinning me around to face him.

"Georgia, please. I'm not trying to freak you out. But if you are actually seeing what you say you are, that's the only explanation. It's not something you can turn on and off, it's just something you *are*. You don't have to be afraid of it."

"I'm a witch, like my evil witch mother?" I snap. "Then why am I seeing this stuff now? Why not my whole life?"

Luke frowns. "It has to be a spell. You had a spell on you that made it so you wouldn't see what you're supposed to see. In that case, the incantation I gave you would have taken it off. Your mom must have done it, that would explain—"

"My mother was not a witch!" I yell. "Stay away from me!"

I throw up my hand to him, palm forward. It's a strange motion, but in that moment of rage, it feels right. "Don't ever talk to me again."

I turn, and this time Luke doesn't stop me. I don't even bother going back into school; I just storm around the building to the parking lot. By some miracle, no one is outside to see me, but somehow I had the feeling they wouldn't be. I drive right through town, and I don't stop until I'm grinding the SUV up Gemmie's driveway.

The Sayers Clan

Gemmie's waiting at the door when I slide the SUV to a stop. I yank my keys out, trying to get a handle on the spinning images that flood my mind: when I was sick my mother made us tea from plants she got in the garden, candles she always kept burning in the windows during storms, the way she always could tell when someone was going to call us or show up at our house, how she always knew *exactly* when one of us was going to get hurt...

A memory comes back to me, something that has to be pulled up by the roots, I've pushed it so far down. The night of the fire at my old house. The arsonists running around outside. I hear their shouts, their muffled footsteps as they drench our lawn with gasoline. I remember my mom, pregnant with Abby, standing in the living room, arms spread wide, muttering something. I was five, sitting at her feet as Charlotte and Callie clung to my arms. We weren't even able to open our eyes, much less believe it was happening. The fire ate away the front of our house, but not that room. Somehow, she held it back. Outside, they shouted, *Burn, witch, burn!*

I get out of the car, walking on weak legs toward the cottage. Gemmie looks older than I've ever seen her before. Dark circles discolor the delicate skin under her eyes.

"Come inside, my heart," she says when I reach her, her voice drawn.

"I want to know about Mom," I say, planting my feet. "I want to know about the things I see. They're not hallucinations, are they."

I say it as a statement.

"Tea first, darling." She reaches down to pick up the massive cat that's bumping around her ankles, holding him close as she leads me inside.

I follow, sitting tensely at her kitchen table. She places a teacup in front of me, settling into her chair.

"Yes," she says finally. "Your mother was a witch. I am a witch. *You* are a witch."

She watches my face, waiting for me to fall apart.

I swallow, going to touch the amethyst drop and finding it gone. "Are we evil?"

The question sets her back. She lets out a short, falsetto laugh. "What a question. No, my heart. It's choices that make people evil, not how they're born."

"Why didn't I know? Why did you keep it from us?"

"After the fire, your mother and I decided it was the best decision. She wanted you to have normal lives, to be able to choose paths for yourselves the way a Sayers witch was never able to before." Gemmie runs her hand over the cat's broad head, more to comfort herself than him. "We spelled you and your siblings, to protect you."

"*Spelled*? You put a spell on us?"

She sighs, dipping her head.

"To protect you," she says again.

"The things I see, is that because I'm a witch?" It seemed a cruel joke for a child to have to deal with the visions I'd had my whole life, the stress-induced hallucinations stemming from childhood trauma that I'd been counseled for years on, just because I was born into my family.

"You see omens, just as your mother did. They were something not even our spell could keep from affecting you. They're meant to warn you of things to come. But you must be careful, letting them steer you around. Emily struggled with them her whole life. I think it may have been the reason she joined *Stola Mortem*."

"What's that?"

A sharpness knifes through the middle of her face. "This will be hard. You must remember how much you meant to your mother. She loved you more than you can know."

She's quiet for so long, I'm afraid she's deciding against telling me.

"Is it bad?" I prompt.

"Yes, my darling. It's very bad." She pushes back from the table, winding her way through the kitchen and into her bedroom. When she returns, she has a book under one arm, and a tarnished grey dagger clutched in the other. I barely have time to blink at the strangeness of seeing her with a weapon. When she reaches the table, she circles her hand high, then stabs the blade into the thick wood with such force that it sinks in two inches.

I rocket backward, my chair skittering out from under me. Gemmie says a string of words I can't understand and slowly peels her hand away. The marbled silver hilt begins to ooze a black, smoky substance that globs across the table. A portion rounds out into the shape of a tiny head, as big as an orange. Black, stick-like appendages flail on either side.

It looks like a skeleton, I think.

"This is the man your mother killed."

Frigid confusion grips my chest. I watch the infant sized pitch-creature drag itself an inch at a time across the table, heading toward me. Its spindly little arms keep dissolving and reforming from the tar-like smoke.

I take a step back, still trying process what she said. "*What?*"

"The Sayers coven lived on Inis Mór, one of the Irish Isles, when Emily was a young girl. We come from a very old family, Georgia, which was once very powerful. Very few of us are left now."

Tiny black fingers extend from the creature, reaching for me. I press closer to the wall. At my feet, Gemmie's cat bristles and whines. This can't be real.

"Emily never took to life on the island. It was too small for her. When she was eighteen, she ran away to America. I didn't find her until she was twenty-three and pregnant with Abigail. In the meantime, she'd fallen in love with a man who had convinced her to join *Stola Mortem*, a witch cult. To earn her place, she had to kill this man." Gemmie's gaze ticks over the turbulent black figure. "Another blood witch. This dagger is spelled to trap her victim's essence, keeping him bound to earth forever. It's a brutal fate, even if he deserved it."

She leans forward, grabbing the hilt. As she works it back and forth, loosening it from the table, the black creature is pulled back, further and further, until it's absorbed into the metal. When the last of him disappears, Gemmie pulls the dagger free and pushes it into its sheath.

"We're capable of very dark things, Georgia. You have to be stronger than the part of you that wants to give in to them."

Stronger than the fear.

"Why would Mom want to be a part of that? How could she ever *kill* an innocent person?" My mind rejects the idea. It can't be possible, therefore it doesn't exist.

"This man was not innocent. But *Stola Mortem* doesn't care about that. They care about power, and power is in blood. Emily thought that with enough power, she could change things. She could change the world." Gemmie lays down the dagger, coming around the table to where I'm still shaking against the wall. "She wanted you and your siblings to have power she never had. You have lineage from the two oldest families in our histories. Each of you was birthed on a solstice or equinox. And five is the most powerful number in the craft."

"So what, we're tools?" I swipe the back of my fist over my nose. "That's the only reason she had us?"

"You changed her life, my darling," Gemmie says, taking my chin in her hand so I look at the sincerity in her eyes. "She left the cult for you—to *protect* you."

"What about our father?" Never in my life had I given him a second thought before now. It seemed odd, but Jack Parks, my stepdad, had always been my father. I hadn't needed another one. Gemmie turns away, but not before I see the expression of hate that pulls at her mouth.

"Faolan," she says. It takes me a moment to realize that's his name. "He was from the Sicario family, descendants of the Crowthers. Your parents first met in Louisiana and joined the cult together. Emily left him when she was pregnant with Abigail. She wanted a life for you, away from him and the cult."

"Where is he now?" I ask.

"Dead," she answers stiffly. "Dead and bound. We made sure of that."

I sit back in the chair, my bones hollow. "You didn't tell us to protect us."

Gemmie keeps her back to me, resting her hand on the table. "We did. Though I wonder now if it was a mistake."

We stand in silence for a while, both processing the gravity of Gemmie's admission. The cat is the only one that seems to have brushed off the encounter entirely. He settles across my thighs, kneading his pads into my jeans.

Eventually, Gemmie picks up the book she'd brought from her room. I'd forgotten about it in the commotion. She places it in front of me. At some point it had been leather, though now it's so badly flaked it's hard to tell.

Delicately, I open the cover. On the first page of thick yellow parchment paper, someone's handwritten the name *Emily S. Sayers*. My heart folds in on itself. I clutch the book closer, turning its pages with painstaking care. It's her handwriting.

"This is your mother's diary," Gemmie says. "Staring the day she ran away. She always planned to give it to you one day. She hoped it would explain…"

She doesn't finish.

I come across a blank page halfway through. There are three more in another section. Flipping quickly, I notice whole chunks are missing, some cut off midsentence.

"Why are these blank?" I ask.

"They're not. I spelled them so you can only read them after your eighteenth birthday."

"Why?" I can't keep the crossness from my tone.

They're my mother's words, and I want them all.

"Some things are not meant for children." The way she replies leaves no room for negotiation. "Now I must ask you a question. Why did you lift our spell?"

"I didn't know I was." I pick at the gritty dried cover of the journal. "It was just an incantation to open my mind."

"The spell was meant to lift when you wanted it to," Gemmie says, resting a tired elbow on the table. "When you wanted to see."

"I guess I can't take it back now," I say ruefully.

A glance at my phone tells me it's time to pick up my brother and sisters from school. I stand, feeling like my blood has turned to sand. Gemmie walks me to the door. I hug her, breathing in her scent of lavender and honey. I turn to leave, but stop.

"Should I tell them?" I'm thinking of my siblings. The discovery had come at the cost of my safe, stable world. But if it was part of me, it was part of them.

Gemmie draws in a long breath. "You must. You're most powerful together. I'm afraid something is coming, and they will need to be as prepared as they can be."

Revelations

"Smells great, sister Gee," Wyatt says when I set a big bowl of pasta on the table. I tried to make the most comforting meal I could manage for dinner.

He sticks his fork in it, peering at the noodles closely. "What did you do different?"

"I used some herbs from the garden," I say, spooning some salad onto my plate. Mom had meticulously crafted her herb garden over the years, something we'd neglected to care for once she was gone. It had slowly burgeoned into a shaggy outgrowth, the stronger herbs overtaking the weak, and everything refusing to die.

Abby glances at Dad's empty chair. "Should we wait for Dad?"

"He's running late. Someone had a miscarriage," I answer.

Everyone turns to me, and I blink, wondering where that had come from.

"Did he call?" Abby asks, scrunching her brow.

"He can't call because his phone is dead," I go on slowly.

"Did someone else call?" Abby prompts.

"No, I just know," I say honestly. The answer seems so clear to me. I feel the truth of it, but I can't voice the reason. They all look at me for a second before returning to their food.

"Georgia's being weird," Callie whispers to Charlotte.

"Seriously?" I say loudly. "I'm like a foot away from you."

Callie turns to me, her eyes defiant. "Well, you are. You've never skipped school before, and you acted like it wasn't even a big deal."

"I'm going through some stuff," I say, my voice faltering.

I chug down apple juice to keep myself from breaking down. When the secret comes out, it has to sound real. It can't sound like I'm having one of my "episodes."

"Do you want to tell us about it?" Abby asks sweetly, and I adore her for caring.

"I do. Look, I found out something about Mom. She—"

A shrill ringing cracks out from the house phone in the kitchen. Charlotte slips out of her chair to answer it. Callie watches me through narrowed eyes, and I glare back at her. After a minute of garbled conversation, Charlotte returns, her arms wrapped around her stomach.

"Dad's nurse said he's going to be another few hours. His patient had a miscarriage, and his phone died."

Four faces turn to me.

"Okay, what's going on?" Callie asks stonily.

"What did you find out about Mom?" Charlotte says, as if she hadn't even heard her twin. The way she looks at me, the steady knowledge in her eyes, I can tell she's already guessed it. Out of all of us, Charlotte's always the one who unravels the puzzle first.

"Mom... was a witch."

Not even one muscle moves on anyone's face. "Gemmie's a witch. We're all witches."

A precarious silence paralyzes the air in the house. Callie breaks it first, scraping her chair back in a restricted rush.

"I'm calling Dr. Hoffsteter," she says. "While I'm at it, should I tell him you're hearing voices again, Wyatt? Georgia's breaking out the crazy train, everyone on."

Wyatt puts his fork down, and stares at the table. I wish he was closer, I want to touch his shoulder, to tell him we weren't crazy our whole lives.

"Callie, I'm serious," I say, hoping my words will break through to Wyatt. "The things I've been seeing all my life are omens, they're something only witches see."

Callie clenches her jaw, crossing her arms. "This is so stupid, Georgia."

"*Listen* to me," I say, my voice rising. "It's not something to be scared of, we just *are* witches. We can see and do things. All the medicines Mom made, and what happened with the fire, it's all because she—"

"Stop saying she was a witch!" Callie shouts across the table.

"Callie, shut up," Charlotte says, silencing her twin instantly. "You're only scared because you know it's true."

The two lock eyes, a silent conversation passing between them.

"What does that mean?" Abby's young voice sobers us all. I decide to take a less aggressive approach.

"Mom and Gemmie put a spell on us when we were really little to keep us from knowing we were witches. She wanted us to live normal lives. There's... a lot of crap that comes along with it."

"So we have a spell on us now that keeps us from seeing and feeling things we should be able to?" Charlotte asks.

"Yes. I lifted mine by accident, and everything is different."

"You did *witchcraft*?" Callie uncrosses her arms. "Do you have any idea what Dad would do if he found out?"

"This is more important than house rules, Callie!" I snap, anger pounding in my throat like hot water.

"You're always so reckless, Georgia," she goes on. "You never know when to just butt out and leave things alone."

"Let me freaking *talk!*"

When I shout the last word, and the light above the table bursts, showering down on us in shards and powder. Abby squeals and covers her head, cowering against the back of her chair. Everyone jolts in their seats, then freeze, as if waiting for more.

The rest of the lights are still on, but for some reason, the house feels as wrong and eerie as if we were plunged into pitch darkness. No one knows what to say.

Charlotte finally turns to me.

"Take my spell off too," she says.

Family Ties

We decide to do it in my room. It's a toss up as to when Dad gets home, and we can't risk being caught. Thinking about Dad, with his tired face and deep worry lines, I'm struck with the realization that he must know. We always knew he wasn't our real father, biologically, but I never realized how much of a burden he'd carried with this family. What had he thought about my mother? How must it have felt to raise us, looking at our faces every day and knowing what lurked in our genes? Somehow I couldn't bear the thought of shattering the world he'd worked so hard to create for us.

I fish out the napkin with Luke's incantation, which I'd tucked into mom's journal in my nightstand. The candle is still where I left it on the floor, cemented to the wood with dried wax.

"Right, so, you should probably sit down," I say to Charlotte. Everyone else has chosen a corner of wall to watch us warily.

"What about casting a circle?" she asks.

"Doing a what?" Suddenly I feel horribly inadequate to be doing this.

"It's what you do before you cast a spell. So you're in a protected space and nothing outside can influence you? You draw it with chalk."

I shake my head in wonderment. "Where did you learn that?"

"She reads all those teen witch books," Callie drawls from the corner.

"Well, I didn't use one, but if you want to we can," I tell Charlotte.

"I have some," Abby pipes up. "In my—"

"Backpack, I know," Charlotte finishes, ducking out of the room. She returns with a pack, pulling out a worn white stick. Kneeling on the floor, she spins in a slow circle, dragging the chunk along the floorboards. When it's closed, she sits back Indian-style.

"You have to read this," I say handing her the napkin.

While she reads it over, I light a match to the candle. I sit next to her, my knee just outside the line she's drawn.

"I'm right here," I say. Charlotte nods, closing her eyes and taking a breath through her nose. She's got a better memory than I do. The words come tumbling out of her in perfect order, no hitches. When she gets to "release my soul within," the tiny flame pops, then leaps a foot higher, jerking and quivering in a thick blaze. Charlotte is flung backward as if invisible hands shove her. I wince at her twisted face, remembering the pain I'd felt and wishing I had warned her.

The flame sucks back down to the wick and smolders out. Charlotte sits up, her brow glossed with sweat.

"That sucked," she bursts. "Thanks for telling me—"

Her eyes widen. "Whoa," she says. "You have this cloud around you."

"I know," I grin. The feeling that I'm not in this alone anymore is enough to make me smile for the first time all day. "Apparently it's an aura."

"I feel..." Charlotte presses her palm to her chest, struggling to articulate something. "I feel..."

"I know," I say. "It's like that at first. But eventually the pieces fit right."

"I knew we were different," she says, raising her smoky-lidded eyes to mine. "I felt it. Things always happen to us, you know? Like Melanie Carver, after she left the broom in my locker and told everyone our father was the Devil. I used to sit and just think about her skin drying out and shriveling, and that year she got Ichthyosis and had to leave school."

"Charlotte," Abby breathes, her eyes huge and horrified.

"I want mine off too." Callie steps forward, twisting her hands together. "Sometimes... sometimes I have dreams that come true. I'll see something so vividly, and it always happens. Last night I dreamed you talked to Gemmie, and a ghost came out of a table. She gave you a journal that was Mom's."

I get to my feet, walking to my nightstand. My fingers have trouble gripping the journal as I take it out. When I turn to Callie, her brow collapses, acceptance finally caving her resolve. She takes the journal when I hold it out to her, tears rolling out of her eyes.

"Mom," she says.

"The ghost did come out of a dagger," I tell her. She nods, her gaze locked to the pages as she turns each one as delicately as if they were tissue.

"I want to take my spell off too," Abby says. Her little chin is unwavering in her determination.

We all turn to Wyatt. He shifts under the sudden attention. It dawns on me that he hasn't said a word since I told them the truth. I take a step toward him. "Wyatt. We're in this together now. You're not alone."

"I want to go last," he says flatly.

I blink. We all seem to be coming apart at the seams like old stuffed animals, but he's not even chinked. *Must be a boy thing,* I tell myself. I turn back to Callie, who's already taken her sister's place in the circle.

Callie takes it better than I did, barely letting herself wince at the pain. Abby is the hardest to watch. She squirms and cries when the spell leaves her, her face twisting under the torture of it. When she's finished, she retreats to my bed, hugging my pillow to her chest.

Wyatt still hasn't moved an inch. His hands are hiked up under his arms, and a strange scowl has taken over his expression.

"Just try it, Wyatt," I say gently, holding the incantation out to him. He takes it between to fingers, his back still flush against the wall.

"Get in the circle," Charlotte says.

"I don't want to. Georgia didn't," he snaps.

I haven't seen him this petulant since he was ten and Dad took away his Playstation.

"I didn't," I say. "You don't have to if you don't want to."

He scans over the words a few times, shoving the napkin into his pocket when he's done. He closes his eyes, speaking them in a sloppy, hurried stream. Everyone winces, waiting for the pain to hit him.

He opens his eyes and shrugs. "Sorry. Don't feel anything."

He turns sharply, skirting around the bedframe, and a twitch of movement in his hand draws my eye.

"What were you doing with your fingers?" I say.

His neck goes rigid, like someone jerked his puppet string. He pivots slowly, raising his hands, spreading his fingers wide. "Nothing."

"Let's try it again. One more time." I can hear my big sister voice coming out, the tone that used to be the only thing he'd listen to. But I know I'd seen it. He was crossing his fingers.

He stays still but something moves in his eyes, like shuffling embers.

"No. It's a waste of time," Wyatt says. His voice is low, not the voice of a fourteen-year-old anymore. In fact, looking at him now, I don't see Wyatt at all. All the smooth innocence in his face has turned to jagged anger and distrust. Something about him is off, and I want so badly to put it right again.

"Let's just try it," I say. I don't wait for him to answer. I'm already striding across the room and grabbing both his hands. The minute my skin touches his, cold spasms grip my muscles. I know I can't hold onto him for long, he's a foot taller than me, so out of desperation I yank him forward. He's just off-balance enough to stagger into the circle.

The sound that comes from him tears my heart to shreds. I'd heard him cry before, when he got shots or when he'd broken his arm, but nothing like this. It was the wailing scream of someone in more pain than I'd ever experienced. His shoulder blades pull together, and his spine curves backward, as if someone is dragging a rake down his back.

Abby covers her ears and screams over him, "Georgia, stop it! Let him go!"

My knees finally bend and I rush toward my baby brother. The toe of my sneaker crosses the circle first. Before I get my body past the line, my feet are ripped out from under me. The back of my head smacks floorboards, shooting a white flash across my vision. Blackness creeps in quickly from the corners of my eyes as the lights in the room surge angrily. The last thing I see is Abby and the twins hurl against the far wall like leaves in the wind, and Wyatt, still screaming on his knees in the circle.

Iona

"Where is he now?" Luke asks, pressing the towel-wrapped icepack to my head.

Its coldness seeps through my hair, cradling my throbbing skull. Luckily, I had gotten the worst knock out of all of us. My sisters are jammed on the loveseat across from me, nursing minor bruised elbows and tailbones.

"We don't know," I say. "We were all knocked out, and he was gone when we woke up. He won't answer our calls. I can't believe I forced him into the circle like that."

Luke sits on the coffee table in front of me. It's not the living room I would have imagined him in. It's too colorful, almost whimsical. His aunt and uncle seem to be from much different stock.

"Why did you?" Luke asks.

The silent judgment in his voice makes me feel like I've made another misstep, a serious one this time. Why was I so bad at this? It was supposed to be in my blood.

The ice nips at my brain stem, and I'm almost glad of the pain. It's a fraction of what I deserve. "I don't know why. I just couldn't believe it worked on all of us and not him."

"He was crossing his fingers," Abby says. Her usually musical voice has gone hoarse. In fact, we all seem a bit dampened.

"He was, wasn't he? You saw it too?" I ask her. "What does that mean?"

I turn to Luke. For once, he looks taken aback.

"Are you sure?" he says. "You saw him crossing his fingers?"

I say I did, and my sisters back me up with nods.

"Because that's something only a witch would know how to do."

"Okay, I'm pretty sure every four-year-old can do *this*." I hold up my own intertwined index and middle fingers.

He looks like he desperately wants to sigh at me, but manages to restrain himself. "Yeah, but guess where it comes from? It's a way to ward off spells. If you know someone's aiming a spell at you, cross your fingers. Nine out of ten times that spell won't work."

"But how would Wyatt know that?" I say slowly, rolling the meaning of it all around in my mind.

Luke shakes his head. "Sorry, but I'm done pretending I can tell you anything about your family."

I swallow, taken aback by his tone. Then I remember the last time I'd seen him, I'd screamed at him for trying to tell me exactly what Gemmie had. I open my mouth to apologize, but there's a jangle of noise outside. The wind chimes are tapping together in the breeze. Luke stands up. "My aunt and uncle are home. I'm going to tell them you guys are here."

His long stride carries him into the hall, leaving the four of us alone. Six pairs of identical green eyes stare at me with mixed degrees of distrust. The sibling camaraderie that just an hour ago had been thick as tar seems to have evaporated.

"I didn't mean to hurt him," I say.

"How do you know this guy?" Charlotte asks, tipping her head in the direction Luke went.

"It's complicated." I resituate the icepack. "I tutor him. His family has a background in Wicca and *Brujeria*, he was the one who gave me the incantation."

"He knows about us?" Callie asks. She says it like I've just handed over state documents to a North Korean spy.

"He does now. He didn't at first. It was all kind of a big accident."

"I don't think we get to believe in accidents anymore," Abby says, closing her arms around her thin frame.

The front door shuts, and voices banter back and forth in the hall. A woman bustles into the living room, tossing her jacket blindly onto the floor as she makes a beeline for us. Several strings of gemstone pendants click together as she hustles around the coffee table, pausing directly in front of my sisters. Her momentum is such that her thick black hair keeps swinging even after she's stopped.

"You poor things," she says, touching Abby and Callie on the tops of their heads. "You must be so scared. I'm Iona, Luke's aunt. We'll get you some tea and some bread pudding, everything will seem better. Finn!" She barks at the doorway, where Luke has trailed back in with a middle-aged man, who's watching his wife with knowing amusement. "Get the babies some tea, they're shaking. Which one is Georgia?"

Guiltily, I raise my hand. The woman steps toward me, a warm smile melting across her mouth. "Of course you are. I'd know you anywhere, Luke's spent hours talking about you."

"*Iona*," Luke and Finn say at the same time.

"Let's get them that tea, angel," Finn goes on, extending a hand to her. His patient expression reminds me of my father. Iona swishes off, her long dress hovering just above the floor. Now I know where the style in the house comes from. When they've gone, Luke shoves his hands deep into his pockets.

"Georgia, can we talk?" he asks, his voice low. I nod and stand, handing off my icepack to Abby. Luke silently leads me to the back of the house, past the kitchen where Iona is spooning out an entire pan of bread pudding onto plates. We stop at the last door on the left, Luke stepping back to let me inside.

This room suits him. The Caulfield house isn't big by any accounts, and Luke's room reflects that, but the calmness and simplicity has his touch all over it. Almost everything is white, and his floor puts mine to shame. Not a single dirty shirt or wayward sneaker.

"I hate to tell you, but I think you're a hoarder," I say, noting his lack of possessions.

Besides two books and a lamp, nothing else is on display.

Luke breathes out, and when I look at him, he's smiling.

"Thank you for letting us come here," I say. "I know it was weird for me to ask you, but all the power went out after the circle. And my dad still hasn't come home."

Luke moves over to his bed, leaning against the aged brass frame.

"I'm sorry," I say at last. "You were right. You were trying to help me, and I was horrible to you."

He taps his fingers against his knee, his face somber. "It wasn't just you. I grew up knowing I was a witch, like my parents and my aunts and uncles did. I can't imagine what it would be like to just wake up one day and find out."

"It's not the best day of my life," I say.

"You cursed me, you know." He finally turns those pale eyes to me, and my lungs forget how to function. "When you told me never to speak to you again. Not a strong one, but still. You said it and you meant it, put all your energy into it. I wanted to stop you, but I couldn't talk."

The knowledge is more than I can process. I don't know where to begin deciphering how that works. But I remember how it had felt when I said it, like something had drained from me, chipped off.

"I can't believe I did that." I touch my throat again, wanting to feel the firm stability of the amethyst stone, but it's still gone. Luke pushes off the bed, pulling the silver strand out of his back pocket.

"You need to learn to control your spells," he says, walking toward me. "You can't just be throwing curses around when you're angry or scared."

He clasps the necklace at the back of my neck, and the drop settles comfortably between my collarbones. His finger lingers for just a moment under my ear, grazing the soft skin and making my breath catch.

"Will you teach us?" It comes out unbidden. I'm glad some part of my brain was lucid enough to say "us" and not "me."

Luke makes a sound like half a laugh. "Uh—"

"Nothing complicated. Just show us what we're supposed to know. So we're not so..." I twist the carnelian ring, trying to think of the right word. "Behind."

He glances at the ceiling, weighing things in his mind. "Are you going to get frustrated and curse me again?" He says it teasingly.

I press my hand over my heart. "I won't, I promise."

He chucks me under the chin. "Got you all ready. Promises for witches are binding. Don't throw those around either."

"Good thing you're here then, *sensei*." I glance at my phone, noticing how late it's getting. "We should probably go home. We all have to be sane enough that my stepdad doesn't think anything's going on."

As we walk back down the hall, his aunt swings her head out of the kitchen. I can see the resemblance in their facial shape and coloring, though Luke is fairer. But Iona lacks any of the sharp lines that Luke has.

"Georgia, love," Iona says. "Your sisters just left. Callie took your car."

"She did not," I say before I can stop myself. Callie had missed out on getting her license by a full ten points. She knew better than to get behind the wheel of my car. Luckily the SUV was more boat than vehicle, it could handle a couple knocks.

"I can take you home," Luke says.

Iona curves an eyebrow up to her hairline. "Helmets," she says.

"Always," Luke answers, bending to give her a kiss on the cheek. "G'night."

She opens her arms to me, and I step into them. When she hugs me, it reminds me so much of my mother that for a moment my lungs freeze. Iona seems to sense that I'm tottering on the edge of an emotional breakdown, and brushes a hand over my hair. "You're always welcome here, sweetheart. Anything you need."

Luke pulls his motorcycle up to the curb, leaning its weight onto his left foot. I unwrap myself from his back, my legs instantly missing the contact. I unstrap my helmet, fastening it to the back.

"I'll see you for tutoring tomorrow," Luke says, only his eyes showing from under his helmet. "We'll try Friday night for our first circle. Supposed to be a full moon, we might get some cool stuff going."

"Sounds good," I say, clasping my hands behind my back. "Thank you again. I don't know what I would have done without you tonight."

"You would've been fine. You're a strong one." He nudges me with the toe of his sneaker before rolling the chopper into motion. He waves as he disappears down the street.

I open the front door, gearing up to ream Callie for car theft. The lights are back on, but the house is silent. I pad through the living room, listening for a telltale creak or rustle to let me know where everyone is.

"Hello?" I call. "Callie, I think we need to talk about crime and punishment!"

Bang! Every door on the bottom floor slams shut at once. I jump so hard it sends a lightning bolt through the bruised part of my head.

I'm about to give my sisters an ear-full, to tell them tonight of all nights isn't the time to pull pranks, when the kitchen, bathroom, closet, front and back doors all fly open at the same time and the worst part is, no one is behind any of them.

Bang, bang, bang. They open and close, smashing the air with such noise that I can only cover my ears until it's over.

When they finally stop, settling back into lifelessness, my heartbeat fills my ears with almost as much noise. Was this some kind of omen? If it was, I didn't know how long I was going to last at this witch thing before I had a heart attack.

Movement on the stairs snatches my attention. Callie is crouching on the fourth step, clutching her comforter over her like a parka.

"Um, yeah," she says acidly. "We have a ghost now. This is going really great so far. Yay."

Circle Casting 101

Monday morning, I'm practically catatonic. None of us slept well, between waiting for Wyatt and Dad, and the incessant moaning of the pipes and wood. Whatever had slammed the doors seemed to have been satisfied with its message and crept into the walls.

In the kitchen, I drag myself between the fridge and counter, assembling cereal for myself. I'm too tired to even care about the creaking anymore. Dad weaves around me, pouring coffee.

"I need to get the plumbing checked out," he says when a particularly loud whine comes from the ceiling above us.

I grunt an assent. He gives me a hug around the shoulders and heads out, grabbing toast off the counter. The front door opens a few minutes after he's gone, and I go rigid.

"Wyatt?"

After a painful moment, my brother slumps around the corner into the kitchen. As tired and ragged as I feel, he looks ten times worse. The way he moves, it's like his back is barely strong enough to keep him upright. He leans over the counter, wearily pulling the plate of toast closer.

"I don't want to talk about it," he says coarsely.

"I just want to say I'm sorry. I shouldn't have forced you into something you weren't ready for."

He chews, expressionless. I watch him for the slightest hint of what's wrong. Of all my siblings, he and I have always been on the same wavelength. Maybe it was the hours of child therapy we had to go through together growing up, but I could always read him perfectly. Now, it's like staring at a house with no lights on inside. I keep trying to convince myself his reaction to the circle was out of fear, but the feeling keeps gnawing at me. Something still isn't right.

"Where were you last night?" I say, leaning onto my elbows. "We covered for you with Dad, but still. We were really worried."

"Went to a friend's."

I'm about to press him for details, but a mass the size of a basketball plummets from the ceiling, landing right between us on the counter and smashing into pieces. Wyatt and I reel back, just missing being clipped by flying chunks of pottery. It's one of the fancy serving bowls we keep on the high shelves that line the kitchen wall. Something pushed it off.

Wyatt looks about four, with his wide eyes and gaping mouth. His chest pumps in and out as he tries to catch his breath. In this light, I can't see a trace of what I saw last night. He's just my brother, same round cheeks, same cleft chin.

"What the hell was that?" he splutters.

"This stuff started happening last night when we got home. I think it's a poltergeist."

He throws up his hands. "Perfect. You couldn't just leave it alone, Georgia."

He marches out of the kitchen and I wilt a bit as the refrigerator starts rattling against the wall. With one eye on the ceiling, I sweep up the shattered fragments on the bowl, trying not to think of it as my life.

"I have some ideas," Luke says, laying his backpack on the ground. Callie, Charlotte, and Abby sit on the floor of the living room like three little ducks in a row. All week we'd been planning for Friday, our first real circle. We'd gotten Dad out of the house with bowling coupons for him and his friends, which gives us a few hours of freedom.

Wyatt still wants nothing to do with it. When Charlotte told him what we were doing, he was gone within an hour. I'd stopped trying to make up for the circle. Whenever I reached out to him, all I got was venom and sulking.

Luke starts unloading apple-sized chunks of rough quartz from his backpack, setting them in a pile.

"I figured I'd teach you basic circle casting, then we can get fancy." He waggles his eyebrows at me.

"Are you a *brujo*?" Abby pipes up.

From his expression, she may as well have asked him where babies come from.

"Uh. Yeah, I guess so. That's how I was raised, anyway."

"*Brujos* use animals in rituals, right? Do you kill animals for sacrifices?"

"*Abby!*" I hiss at her.

"It's fine." Luke clears his throat. "No, I don't do that. But my parents did. And my Aunt Idra did, before she went nuts. They did a lot of stuff you don't really want to know about." He finishes heavily, and Abby's smart enough not to press him. He claps his hands, shaking off the somberness. "Right. So before you know anything else, you gotta understand energy. We're powered by energy. We give it off and take it in constantly. So does the earth, but on a much bigger scale. Spell casting is a manipulation of your—or something else's—energy for a specific purpose."

He hands me four chunks of quartz.

"Kindly pass those around, assistant," he says with the voice of a talk show host.

I make a face at him, but dole them out as he picks up a quarter-thick roll of chalk.

"As a witch, you can use certain things to help focus your energy. The quartz is going to help you call up power. I want to see what I'm working with." He rises to a half crouch, dragging the chalk along the ground in an arc behind us.

"Circles are spaces that you create. Negative energy can't cross chalk, same with salt, so it's safer inside the circle."

Wyatt. I can't help the thought, and instantly I'm ashamed all over again.

"When you get really good, you can create circles for different purposes, like if you don't want a particular person to cross it. But if you do it wrong, it can hurt someone."

Everyone turns to me. I chew my lip, trying not to remind them all that the first circle wasn't even my idea.

Luke goes on, cutting between us to draw a star. "All right, now you say something like I cast the circle for blah-da-blah, whatever you want to do. We're going to use this one to get your spirit to manifest. When we know what it is, we can work on getting rid of it."

SPELLED

I meet my sisters' eyes, my same apprehension mirrored on their faces. Luke holds out his hands, closes his eyes in concentration. A hushed flow of Spanish tumbles out of his mouth, deep and alluring. I have to hide the smile that fights its way across my lips. When he's done, he directs us to each take a point of the pentagram, setting our crystals at our feet. He places the chalk stick in the center. He has us join hands, taking Abby's and mine. The rough underside of his palm feels warm against my fingers, and a shiver slips between my shoulder blades.

"Since I know the most spells, I'll say the words. Everyone else just focus on what I'm saying and try to imagine calling energy into yourself. And don't be scared. It can't hurt you in the circle."

"I'm not so sure," I grumble.

Luke squeezes my hand. "It'll be okay."

He closes his eyes, and we all do the same. His voice breaks the stillness of the room.

"Spirit, friend or foe,
Cross our circle and speak to us.
We call you across the spirit world.
Reveal your name to us."

Silence falls over the room like a heavy veil. I feel Luke's hand in my left, Charlotte's in my right, both growing warmer and warmer. With no sight to anchor myself, my body seems to float, like I'm suspended in water. Excitement, or maybe fear, spirals up in my chest, rising into my shoulders and lifting me. Curious, I open my eyes to peek.

The crystals are floating. They form a ring in front of us, all quivering in the air at chest level. My head snaps to Luke, and he's looking at me with equal bewilderment. His lips part, about to speak, but then the chalk twitches. It rolls back and forth, then jerks upright. Painfully slow, like a child learning to write, it scrawls a line, then another.

Abby breathes in sharply, hearing the scratching against the wood. I can't look away until the chalk drops back into lifelessness.

In jagged, mismatched letters, the ghost has written: MATTHEW TOWNSEND.

Letters

I can't help it. I try to be stronger than the fear, but it flattens me like a wave, throwing me back against the sand. I'm ripped backward, my hands torn from Luke and Charlotte's as the crystals clatter to the ground.

A shattering sound crashes down on us. Everyone ducks as one by one, the glass picture frames on the wall explode into splinters. Luke shakes my shoulders, cupping my face in his hands, blocking out everything but him.

"Georgia, you're fine. Calm down. Breathe."

I nod, trying to suck in a breath that doesn't make it to my lungs.

"You pulled too much energy," he says, "and it's trying to find an outlet. Just let it go. Breathe and let it go."

I exhale, my body deflating. My heart stops drumming as insistently, slowly accepting that we aren't in danger. The last picture frame swings on its nail, cracked, but intact. Luke helps me stand up.

"Jesus, Georgia," Charlotte says, her cheeks still red with breathlessness.

"Um." Callie points to the writing on the floor. "Did we talk to the ghost?"

Luke walks back into the circle, peering down at the message for the first time. I can almost feel the weight pressing down at him as he stares at the name, his face clouding.

"Matthew?" he says, barely a mutter. "Matthew, is that you?"

We all wait for a sound, a creak, anything, but the house is lifeless again.

"I'm sorry." Luke grinds his fist into his chest, over his heart, his voice twisted with such pain it makes my throat close. "I'm sorry I didn't protect you."

At the corner of the room, the metal vent in the ceiling clatters to the ground. Out of the hole, a rectangular box plummets down, landing squarely on the floor. Charlotte wastes no time marching up to it, while the rest of us stay motionless, as if we're afraid it might charge us.

Charlotte lifts up a faded shoebox, barely held together by leather strings wrapped around it. She brings it over to the circle, setting it on the floor and gingerly removing the ties like a surgeon.

"If there's a skull in there, I'm out of here," Callie states.

The lid comes off, and Charlotte pulls out a handful of cream envelopes.

"Letters," she says. She paws through the box, setting out two more bundles.

"Are they Mom's?" I ask.

"Got to be," Charlotte says, opening one and unfolding the paper inside. "But it's not her handwriting."

I take the sheet from her. It's stiff and thick, old paper that's done it's time with dust. I peer at the handwriting, coming to the same conclusion. Mom's handwriting was a constricted, almost Edwardian cursive, a product of her British upbringing.

"Why would she hide these?" I wonder aloud.

"Why did the ghost want us to find them?" Charlotte adds.

"Not a ghost. Matthew Townsend," Abby says, her voice uncharacteristically serious. She looks at Luke, who doesn't seem to be fully with us anymore. "Did you know him?"

"Yeah, I knew him. He died in the fire at Sagestone High. He's," he says softly before correcting himself, "he *was* my friend."

"Why's he in our house?" Callie demands.

Luke shakes his head, swallowing hard. "I don't know. But it's not a good thing. If he hasn't moved on, there's a reason for it. Sorry, guys. This took a lot out of me. I'm going to head home. We'll do this again next Friday." He slings his backpack over his shoulder. "I'll be more… prepared."

He stalks past us, veering to the left, down the hall. My chest constricts as soon as I hear the front door close, and I know I can't leave it like this.

I catch him in the front yard as he's strapping his backpack to his bike. "Luke!"

He turns to me, and I almost don't recognize him. He's carrying such a burden, it's drawing down the corners of his face.

"I'm so sorry," I say. "I know what it's like to lose someone."

"Do you know what it's like when it's your fault?" he says bitterly, like each breath is tearing into him. "When you could have stopped it, and you didn't because you were too stupid to see it coming? I knew what he was getting into, and I thought I could save him by myself, but I couldn't. It's my *fault*." His voice cracks on the last word. "Mine."

I wrap my arms around his shoulders without even thinking. I just can't stand there and watch him break apart on the sidewalk. He rests his head against my neck, his hands crossing over my back, holding onto me like the world is spinning and I'm the only stable thing in it.

"I do know," I say quietly into his shirt. "My mom killed herself."

He stiffens, his arms tightening around me. "Jesus. I'm sorry."

I pull away, feeling the abhorrent sting in my eyes that preludes tears. "It's okay. We're all fine now. I just wanted you to know, we're a bit damaged too."

Luke nods, forcing his mouth into a tiny smile. It's a feat, given the night we've had.

"It gets better than this," he promises. "We're going to find a way to help him, then I'm going to show you the beautiful parts of the craft."

"Good, because I'm not really sold on it yet," I say heavily.

Luke throws a leg over his chopper. With his first finger, he taps me under the chin.

"See ya, kid."

He pulls away from the curb, rumbling down the street. I wait another moment in the warm darkness of the night. Somehow it's soothing to be outside, away from the cold starkness of the house, and the dead boy's spirit creeping around in our walls. I'm steady my breathing, counting heartbeats, when something lands in the mesquite tree above me, beating strong wings against the air. I look up, hoping maybe it's one of the barn owls we get in the fall.

A white face looks down, vast eyes like black glass fixed on me. I take a step back. It's by far the creepiest bird I've ever seen. It's the size of a vulture, with the same unforgiving beak, but its face is flat like an owl's. The rest of its body could be beautiful, with feathers the color of milky tea cloaking its chest, growing darker as they reach its wingtips. But the eyes throw me.

It stares at me, motionless and without even a trace of fear. It's almost human, the way it's sizing me up.

"Georgia." Abby's voice comes from the front door. "Is everything okay?"

"I think I'm seeing an omen," I say. I don't dare break the staring contest, as I've spotted her claws. Four thick curved daggers that are meant for tearing things apart in record time.

"The bird?" Abby says, coming out onto the porch. "I see her too. What is it?"

"I don't know."

She spreads her wings, and I almost duck. They take up at least three feet on either side of her. She sweeps them twice, and she's gone. I shake it off, walking back toward the house.

Charlotte's emptied the box, sorting letters and envelopes into three piles. Callie sits cross-legged next to her, peering at a page full of scrawling, spiky script.

"Do we know what they are yet?" I say.

"It's letters between these two people 'Salem' and 'Isolda.' If those are their real names. Honestly I'm not convinced," Charlotte says. "They're talking about some kind of spell, I think. They call it *Veri Segno*. There's this entire letter on directions for making ink."

She holds out a page to me. I read through it, my skin turning cold.

"Not ink," I say. "Blood. This is how to make ink out of blood."

The twins put on the exact same expression of distaste.

"Why?" Callie says.

The antique lamp in the living room trembles violently, the ceramic clattering against the table underneath. Before any of us can react, Abby marches into the center of the living room, fists clenched.

"Matthew, *enough*!" she bellows with all the might she can muster. "Stop breaking our stuff! If you want to communicate with us, do it with the lights like a civilized ghost."

Immediately, the shaking stops.

"Thank you," Abby says.

The twins and I share impressed glances, not daring to interrupt Abby's roll.

"Obviously, he knows something important is in those letters," Abby says, turning to us. "He wanted us to find them. Is that right, Matthew? Blink the lights once for yes, twice for no."

We wait on our toes for a moment. The lamp flickers once.

"Do you know what this ritual is?" I hazard, holding up the page.

The lamp blinks *yes*.

"Does it have something to do with our mother?" I go on.

Nothing.

"Maybe he doesn't know?" Abby guesses.

"He was friends with Luke. Does it have something to do with Luke?"

Yes.

I sink to the floor, peering at the letter closely. It's from Salem to Isolda, dated 1992.

"I know the Veri Segno will work, it's just a matter of finding the right binding symbols," Salem writes. *"Without being bound to the body, the blood will be useless."*

I turn the paper over. Isolda has written back with half a page of drawn symbols, each connected to the other in a continuous line. It's as beautiful as it is frightening. They seem to swim under my sight, moving with their own energy. I may know nothing else, but I know these drawings are powerful. They're meant for a purpose so far over my head I can't begin to guess at it.

Across the room, Callie lets out a strangled breath. Her hand covers her mouth as she reads the letter she's holding.

"I know what the *Veri Segno* is," she says.

"The ritual?" Charlotte asks, leaning over to look at her page. "What is it?"

"It's meant to steal a blood witch's power. You kill them and drain their blood. Then you mix it with ashes from Yew bark and tattoo it into your body. This guy Salem invented it."

She tosses the paper down, pressing her hand against her forehead.

"I feel sick," she says.

"Why would Mom have these letters?" Abby asks.

Their voices echo around my head hollowly. I can only think of one thing: Luke's tattoos. They can't be. But the strange color, the symbols...

"Matthew," I say, "did Luke do the *Veri Segno*?"

Shock buffets the air in the room.

"What?" Callie says.

"Georgia, what are you saying?" Charlotte seconds her twin.

"I'm asking Matthew."

For so long, I stare at the light, willing him to say no.

Finally, Matthew blinks *yes*. My ribs collapse on themselves, crushing my lungs. All this time, he had looked at me and lied to my face. He'd carried the death of an innocent person in the back of his mind, and still been able to laugh, to smile, to make jokes. Was he really a monster? A murderer?

I stare down at the letter in my hands, the lines muddling together. I move my thumb, noticing a stamp in the left corner. The paper is charred under it, like it has been branded. The mark consists of a tiny bird with outstretched wings. Holding a scythe.

"I know this symbol," I breathe.

It was the same one that had been splashed over the front of Oggun.

"This has to be some sort of sick cult," Charlotte says, sifting through the stack. The symbol is burned into every single one. I run to my backpack, pulling out Mom's journal. The pages flip roughly in my fingers as I pray to find nothing. But there it is. The mark has been burned into the back cover. I slowly turn to my sisters.

"Not just any cult," I say. *"Stola Mortem."*

It's all slotting together in a horrible, nightmarish truth: Luke's parents, my parents, the man at Oggun, why Luke had seemed so familiar, all tied together by the same evil. Abby was right. We weren't allowed to believe in accidents anymore.

My sisters all look up, waiting for an explanation. I swallow, scraping moisture down my dry throat.

I say, "I think it's time I told you the truth about Mom."

Beginner's Curse

I catch a glimpse of myself in the warped mirror hanging in my locker. The weekend wasn't kind to me, and it shows. Luke called everyday, each time its own torture session, seeing his name and experiencing the devastation all over again. My body was reflecting the slow mental deterioration I'd been going through since the day I lifted my spell.

"Georgia."

I've been preparing internally for days, but Luke's voice still slithers down my lower back. When I turn, he's standing behind me in a dark blue sweatshirt, pushed up to his elbow, his hair still wet from swim practice.

"I called you all weekend. I was worried about you guys. Is everything okay?"

There's actual concern in his eyes, which only makes the betrayal more vicious. The entire speech I had prepared evaporates in my mind.

I say the only thing I can think of. *"Veri Segno."*

If there was a small part of me holding onto the hope that he didn't know anything, it dies when he drops his arms, his eyes widening. "Where'd you hear that?"

"So that's it then. Your tattoos. You killed a blood witch and stole her power."

He shifts his eyes to the crowded hallway, shuffling from foot to foot.

"Georgia, we can't talk about this now," he whispers. "Please let me come over and I'll explain it. It's not what you think."

There's only one thing I need to hear him say.

"Are those tattoos *Veri Segno*?" It's a miracle I can keep my voice steady.

He swallows. "Yes."

"Then there's nothing to explain." I reach out and grab his forearm. Studying Mom's journal had taught me that this was the one and only way to make sure a curse got to the person it was meant for. "I may not know what I'm doing, but I want you to look in my eyes and see how much I mean this. *Never talk to me at school again. Do not ever come to my house. Stay away from my sisters and my brother.*"

His face goes slack. Something stuck, even if it was just a beginner curse. My hands shake with the gravity of what I've just done. I slam my locker, shoving my way through the crowd. No sound follows me, but I feel his eyes on my back until I turn the corner.

"Why aren't you at tutoring?" Taylor asks me at lunch. Her baby blue eyes narrow as she looks up at me.

I set my tray down next to M.C.

"I just didn't want to go today," I say stiffly. "Why, is it a problem?"

"Yes," Taylor answers with convincing sincerity, "this is when Gallagher, M.C., and I have our threesomes, and now you've messed it up."

I laugh, relaxing a bit. I couldn't risk Luke showing up and trying to talk to me during our usual period. I wasn't sure how long my spell would last, since the last one was only a couple of hours. I don't know how strong I am, but I'm pretty sure Luke's stronger.

I take his ring off my finger, and instantly the world jumps into a riot of colors. I close my eyes for a moment, telling myself I'm not going to be afraid of it anymore. This is who I am. I'm going to live with it.

When I open my eyes again, everything has dulled to a gentle glow. I let the ring rest in my palm. I'd worn it since the day he gave it to me, even when it burned my heart to look at it. The only way to get it back to him was Taylor. She didn't know what an awkward situation was.

"Could you do me a huge favor?" I ask her, holding out the ring to her.

She takes it, studying it inquisitively.

"Can you give that to Luke? He forgot it," I say, "and I don't want to give it to him."

Taylor nods, slipping it into her shorts pocket.

"So he proposed then?" she says with a grin.

"We actually kind of had a fight," I say.

It strikes me this is the first time I've lied to her in our years of friendship. But *I* can hardly get my head around what's happened with my family. I'm not even sure I could explain it to her.

"Really? Like a lovers' spat?" Taylor cranes her neck around the lunchroom until she spots where he's sitting. "Ugh, Alison is after your man. Like, *all* after your man."

Everyone glances to their table, but I keep my eyes forward. Seeing Luke with Alison is the last thing I can handle right now. I scratch my neck as a tingle runs up it, like fingers softly dragging along the nape.

"He's looking at you," Taylor says, looking directly behind me at Luke's table. "He's full on staring at you."

I shift my shoulders, feeling invisible fingers brush across them.

"He looks miserable," M.C. says.

"Good."

Taylor raises her eyebrows. "Wow, I've never seen bitter Georgia before. What a tiger. I have something to cheer you up though! Guess what we're doing for Halloween?"

"Halloween? That's in like three weeks," I say.

"Yeah, but the awesomeness cannot be contained. We're all driving down to Austin to go to a Full Moon Party at Barton Springs! Excitement is now acceptable."

"Ehh," I say.

"*Ehh*? Okay, your lack of excitement is excused based on your boy issues. But by Halloween, you better have some enthusiasm."

I tear off a piece of sandwich, wondering if I'll ever feel enthusiastic about anything ever again."

The Dead-Blood Curse

When I get home, I go straight upstairs to my bed, pulling out Mom's journal. It's been my only comfort the past few days. It's mainly a collection of spells she'd either created or come across, but occasionally she'd add a note for context. I lived for those. Seeing what she was doing, where she was.

I trace her name on the first page, feeling the loops as if I'm writing it myself. *Emily S. Sayers.* She wasn't that much older than me when she started this journal. I let the book fall open to where I stopped, a recipe for spelled hazelnut tea, meant to keep omens from coming at night.

I turn the page and freeze. It's the first time I've seen my father's name on a page.

Faolan taught me this. I've never seen such intricate circle casting. He's clearly next in line to be leader.

I turn the page. There it is again, that name.

Faolan taught me to spell a dagger. I have to use it for initiation. I worry that I'm not strong enough to do this, but I have no choice. I'll die if I can't be with him.

The spells that follow grow darker, stranger. One calls for the head of a coyote, in order to call a storm over a specific location. A curse to make someone's feet grow sores, *for the bastards that killed my little cat, Penny.*

The next mention of Faolan is under a new house cleansing ritual. *Faolan and I moved into a little cottage on Fisher St. There's a room to put the baby when she comes.*

The baby. That's me. Tears leap to my eyes as I look at the word. Hungrily, I turn the next page, and almost throw the book in frustration. Blank. It wasn't fair for Gemmie to keep parts of my life from me, things I needed to know to be whole.

The next entry I can read is far at the back. It's just an herbal blend for tea.

Helps with paranoia, my mother's written. *Calms nerves. Tasteless. F. doesn't notice when I brew it with his Earl Grey.*

There's a drawing on the next page, something that looks like a slab of rock balanced on two pillars. The entirety of its face is covered with symbols.

F. is making a Cutter Stone.

I put my fingertip over the letter. Somewhere along the way, my father became just "F."

He thinks I don't know about it, but I've seen him carving the marble in the barn. Even if he's powerful enough to craft one, it won't be finished for years. I want to ask him whom he's planning to sacrifice, since the blood must come from a member of your family. And his has died out, besides the children and me. How can he want immortality if it means we can't be together?

Immortality. Could that even be possible? A cold chill climbs down my back. Had Faolan been planning to sacrifice one of us to get it?

They found me, the top of the next page reads. *They find me no matter where I go. F. has them so wrapped up in his lies, they'd throw themselves on a fire if he asked them to. I can't keep running anymore. They'll keep coming for the children if I can't find a way to hide them. There has to be a way to stop all this.*

With heavy fingers, I turn the last page. It's a curse.

The Dead-Blood Curse. There's a list of ingredients, horrible things like hearts of doves and a snake's stomach, that make up some sort of brew. *Once drunk, only an hour of life remains. There won't be any going back. The Cutter Stone will be good one, with his skill. It'll only take the blood of a family member. He's stupid to forget I'm his family too, bound to him by the laws of his own religion. The stone will work once, and F. will take the curse along with my life. One sacrificed soul buys eternity from his God. What kind of god is that, who takes immortality so lightly? Maybe his soul can live forever, but his body will die with me. There is no better end for us, none more deserving of the things we've done. I can die for my children. He can die for his greed.*

"No!" The scream rips out of me before I can stop it, and I fling the book away from me. I all ready feel it again—the way the universe tore in two when we heard she was dead—and I don't want to. I *can't*.

"Your mother killed herself," the worst police officer in the history of police officers had said, "slit her wrists in a backyard in Louisiana. Probably a mental breakdown, due to her history."

Who even *says* that to a kid, much less four kids? Even then I knew it couldn't be true. Whatever a Cutter Stone was, it needed the death of a family member to work, and apparently Faolan was depraved enough to try to one of his own children. The only thing that had saved us was Mom. She'd *sacrificed* herself for us. The knowledge feels like concrete in my stomach.

My door swings open and Charlotte runs in. Right away she knows something's wrong.

"What?" She sinks onto the bed in front of me. "What happened?"

"She died for us. Mom did." The words tumble out of me. I can't hold the hurt in anymore. "Faolan, our father, he was going to kill one of us, and Mom took our place. She cursed her blood and sacrificed herself to kill him."

"I don't understand. Who wanted to kill us?"

I push the journal into her hands. Sobs pummel my insides, too strong to speak through. I watch her face as she reads, follows the same threads until the last page.

"Mom," she whispers when she finishes. "She *saved* us."

"Why would she fall in love with someone like that?" I say, dragging my knuckles over my eyes to stop the flow. "How could she be so blind about him?"

"You don't think you did the same thing with Luke?" Charlotte says, not even looking at me. Her face is stone, closed off. I open and close my mouth, her statement lodged in my heart. It's true. I didn't see because I didn't want to see.

"Where do you think he is now?" Charlotte asks. "Immortal soul with no body. What happened to him? You think he's stuck somewhere, like Matthew?"

All I can do is shake my head. This world we've opened is too big for me. There are a million things I don't understand, and all of them can hurt me.

"Gemmie said they 'bound' him. Maybe he's trapped somewhere, like the soul in Mom's dagger," I say.

Charlotte gathers the journal to her chest. "We have to tell the others. They deserve to know why she left us."

When she leaves, I fall back on my pillows. The one person who might understand this pain, who might be able to explain the chaos we've been thrown into, is the one person I can never speak to again.

Watchers

The bird is back. She's watching as I take the trash out one Sunday, perched in the same u-shaped branch. That strange, pale face tracks my progress down the sidewalk, the two coal orbs of her eyes never blinking. I glare back, replacing the lid of the trashcan.

"Go away," I say.

Her head ticks right, then left, almost mockingly. I turn my back on her, heading inside.

Sundays became our circle nights. Using Mom's journal, we cast simple spells, things with no chance of backfiring. We spelled a protection sachet for Dad's car, using herbs from the garden. We tried to get more answers out of Matthew, but it was hard when the only possible responses were *yes* or *no*.

Today, we're using one of Mom's oldest spells to try to get Abby's crush to ask her out. We spread our supplies out on the floor of my room. It's the furthest from Dad's room, on the opposite corner of the first floor. Abby's tongue pokes out of her mouth as she cuts out a picture of her crush of the month.

"This feels a little stalker-y, Abby," I say, unwrapping a brand new red wax candle.

"What's the point of being witches if we can't make our lives a little better," she says, laying the photo on the ground proudly.

The peal of the doorbell echoes through the house.

I blow out a breath, standing. "I'll get it."

"Be fast!" Abby calls after me.

I open the door on a kid about Wyatt's age, but half as tall and twice as wide. He looks like someone squashed him down with the bottom of a shoe.

"Hi." He grins at me, showing two rows of pointy teeth where not a single one is in the right place. "Is Wyatt home?"

"Who are you?" I say. I can't explain it, but my insides were set squirming the second I saw him.

"I'm his best friend," the kid says, "Keir."

His coloring is agonizingly similar to Luke's, but his eyes are so dark and black, I can't tell where the iris ends and the pupil begins. It's like looking down into two tiny, never-ending wells.

"His best friend is Bradley Smith," I say coldly.

"Things change," the kid says as he chews the inside of his cheek. "Can you just get him?"

I'm about to tell the kid to come back later, but Wyatt's hand grasps the door, pulling it open.

"Come inside," he says to Keir.

"Dad doesn't want company on school nights," I mumble to Wyatt.

"It's fine," he snaps.

"Do you even know this kid?"

For the first time, Wyatt peers right into my eyes, and I step away from him. His gaze is icy, so unlike Wyatt at all that I don't even recognize him for a moment.

The door slips out of my hand before I even realize it. Keir takes the opportunity to shuffle in, but I can't look away from Wyatt. I'm afraid to even blink, until he turns away from me.

The pair trudges up the stairs, not even talking to each other. Keir turns his head over his shoulder, giving me a salute and another toothy grin. I press my hand to my chest, trying to tell myself how irrational I was being. Maybe he was spiraling into something I couldn't touch, but he was still my brother.

"Who was it?" Charlotte asks when I close the door to my room.

I join them in the circle they've drawn, closing it with the chalk and sitting down. "Some creepy friend of Wyatt's."

The mood plummets, making the air in the circle cold. Wyatt had been shunning us since the first circle, slinking around the house in silence, disappearing after school for hours. He'd even quit football. It wasn't like him. But then, nothing these days really seemed like him.

We all hold hands, casting the circle like Luke had taught us to, stating our purpose outright. We assemble the parts of the spell, Abby writing her name over the boy's picture, Callie filling a mason jar with honey, and Charlotte lighting the candle. Everything's handed to me, and I submerge the picture in the jar, twisting the lid and sealing it with wax. I place it in the center. I still haven't gotten over the shudder of fear in my chest every time we call energy. Our voices blending together when we speak the spell sounds like a scene from a movie, when people are calling up the Devil.

I feel a familiar tingle working up my spine, the sensation of waves gently floating under me. I open my eyes just to peek.

The jar is spinning slowly on its rim, but that's not what grabs my attention. Keir is standing in my open doorway, watching us with the expression of a cougar stumbling upon a hurt deer.

I suck in a breath, startled, and the jar explodes. A shard rockets across the circle, burying itself in Abby's shin. She lets out a cry, breaking hands with Callie and Charlotte. The room turns into a vacuum, like someone's blown a hole in an airborne plane, dragging us all toward Abby. She's pulling too much power.

Before I can reach her, the windows burst open, smacking against their sills. Wind pours in, so strong it's as if we're in the middle of a tornado. Papers and books fly off my shelves, ripped from the shelves in the tumult.

"Abby!" Callie throws her arms around our little sister, rubbing her shoulders to calm her down. As she catches her breath, the wind peters out, everything settling across my floor. Abby whimpers softly, examining her injury.

I whip around to look at Keir.

He's unflinching, as if he's seen it a hundred times. The light in his eyes gives me the sick feeling we've just done something very wrong.

"Cool," he says.

The door slams shut on him, taking his leering face away. My bed scrapes across the floor, screeching in protest, and hurls into the wall, blocking the doorway.

"Matthew, stop!" Callie orders. "You know you can't do that when Dad's in the house!"

The ceiling begins to groan and wail, pipes beating against pipes in a loud percussion.

"We get it, you don't like Keir," I hiss. "I don't either."

The whining of the house slowly falls off as Matthew loosens his grip. I leave my bed where it is, thankful for the barrier it makes between the unsettling boy and us.

"He *saw* us," Charlotte says. "What do we do?"

"I don't know," I say, "but I definitely don't think it was the first time he's seen magic."

Halloween

"Okay, so I know my driving record doesn't inspire much confidence," Callie says to me over pizza.

"None at all," I say.

She rolls her eyes. "Fine, but as it *is* Halloween, and you're the best big sister in the world... so please let me borrow the SUV to go to Shannon's!"

Dad bustles into the kitchen, rifling under papers for his keys.

I take a huge bite, trying to hurry through my meal.

"I'm still mad about the last time you took my car," I say, swallowing way too quickly. "Remember, when you left me at Luke's? Besides, I'm going to Austin to meet Taylor and Gallagher. I have to take it."

Callie turns her pout on Dad. "Dad, please take me to Shannon's. None of my friends can drive yet. It's my only chance to do something fun tonight."

"Sorry, honey, I'm headed to the hospital. One of my patients went into premature labor, we're having to do an emergency C-section." He digs his keys out from under Abby's lunchbox.

"That's horrible," I say.

He shakes his head. "Totally healthy mother, never had any problems. Must just be a Halloween curse."

Callie and I look at each other, not sure whether to count that as a joke or not. Dad gives me a kiss on the forehead.

"Be back at eleven. I'm not sure when I'll be home, but it's still a school night."

As he hurries out the front door, Callie sighs exasperatedly. "*Fine*, I guess I'll be a loser and stay home all night."

"Everyone else is home," I say, tucking a slice of pizza up in a paper towel. I'm late meeting Taylor at Barton Springs already. "Have a fun circle with Matthew. Tonight's supposed to be the night the veil between our world and the spirit world is thinnest." I raise my eyebrows suggestively. "Maybe we can finally see what he looks like."

"I know what he looks like. His picture was on the news," Callie grumbles. "Über dork."

The blender turns on furiously.

"She didn't mean it, Matthew," I say, punching the off button. "I gotta go. See you in a few hours. Happy Halloween!"

"Yeah, yeah." Callie slumps into a chair while I rush out the door.

Barton Springs is a strange construct, half nature and half manmade. Apparently M.C. had given Taylor the idea to throw the party at a natural spring the size of three Olympic pools, one with a huge concrete square laid down around it.

The sloping hills on either side of it crawl with people in swimsuits. They all seem to be Sagestone kids.

I sit on the side of the spring, dangling my feet in the frigid water. Taylor joins me, passing me a purple plastic cup filled with grape juice.

"Blood of the ancestors." She bares her teeth in a lion's grin.

I try not to give away the weighty, sick feeling the idea gives me. Gallagher drops down on my other side, letting out a long howl. Everyone around us picks up the call, and soon the entire park rings with the forlorn sound.

"It's tradition," he says to me. "I did my homework."

"We should dance!" Taylor insists. "We need to distract Georgia from the horribleness in her life."

I snort. "Thanks."

"I concur," Gallagher says, standing and heaving me up by my elbow. "'When all else fails, we dance.' Stephen Hawking said that."

"I'm not sure you have the right Stephen Hawking," I say, but the pair is already pulling me toward the circle of bouncing dancers. Gallagher launches into his shockingly-accurate-yet-still-out-of-place-80's-moves, while Taylor reenacts some sort of kickboxing routine. I do my best to smile and bob along, even joining in the next howl when the clouds part and moonlight washes over the grass.

I sway a bit as my mind fills with a light fog. I peek at my drink, wondering if I could possibly have gotten a spiked cup by accident. My body seems to get heavier by the second. Prickling warmth scurries up my limbs, like getting into a hot bath after being very cold. Taylor claps her hands in front of my face, giving me a sharp slap of clarity. I stare at her blearily, her face swimming in and out of focus.

"You okay?" she asks.

"Totally," I answer, sounding much louder in my own head. "I'm going to go to the bathroom."

I push away and weave through the crowd. Somewhere along the way, my drink slips out of my hand. The crowd thins as I trudge along the fence line, until the thumping beat of music has almost faded. My eyes land on a pair of shoes, attached to legs, connected to a body that's blocking my path.

Luke stares down at me, his blue eyes almost glowing in the hazy light.

"Hi," I say hesitantly. I should be angry at seeing him. I should scream and run away. All I can feel is a slightly pulsing numbness.

Slowly, my muffled mind puts the pieces together. "Did you spell me?"

I'm proud of the shred of anger I manage to conjure, despite my body feeling like it's stuffed with cotton.

Luke cracks a very small, apologetic smile. "You didn't really leave me a choice. You won't talk to me. I knew if you saw me, you'd run away."

"You're not supposed to be able to talk to me," I protest. It'd been three weeks since I'd heard his voice. I'd almost forgotten what it sounded like.

"Not at school or your house," he says. "Right now, we're at neither. The problem with curses is you have to be specific."

"How did you know I'd be here?"

"Taylor told me. I asked her if there was any place I might catch you outside of school." I remind myself to give Taylor a lesson in loyalty later.

"This isn't fair," I say.

Luke drops his smile, backing off instantly. "I know. I'm sorry. I really came here to explain."

He takes my hand, tugging me inside the stone building that houses the bathrooms. We slip into the unisex room, the only thing remotely private, wedged in the corner. He closes the door, and I maneuver myself onto the sink, pressing my cheek against the cool mirror.

"This is romantic," I say coldly.

"I know you're afraid of me," Luke says.

"You're a murderer." I start flipping through recollections of every spell I've seen, trying to think of some way to break his curse. I focus on the feeling of glass against my skin, staring at the tiles in the wall until the fuzziness fades slightly.

Luke cups my face in his hands, shaking it roughly so the clouds clear out of my eyes.

"I'm not," he says. "I never killed anyone. You can't know what it was like, growing up knowing that no matter what you do, someone else had just been given more power that you'd ever have."

"Totally. So it was justified. Let me out of here." I try to get my legs under me, but end up crashing sideways into the wall.

Luke hooks my arm, setting me onto the toilet. When he leans down, his eyes are even with mine. That sad face makes a reappearance, begging me to believe that it's seen more horrors than I could ever imagine.

"I told you my parents were evil. They *are* evil. They've been obsessed with power since way before I was born, it's like an addiction to them. My mother is the leader of a cult called *Stola Mortem*. They search out blood witches and perform the *Veri Segno* to steal their abilities. When I was thirteen, they made me go through it. I didn't kill the witch, but I didn't stop it either. I couldn't. You have to understand, I lived my whole life with the cult, I didn't know how to say no. My mother is very powerful. She can make it so you can't fight back."

The muscles in his jaw tighten and shift. *He's afraid of her*, I realize.

"That's the reason I ran away. I didn't *want* the *Veri Segno*. I would give anything to undo it. Her blood is in me now, I can't change that. But I'm not evil, and being tattooed against my will doesn't make me that way."

My mind is fighting, pushing the murkiness back. The room becomes more distinct with every passing second. I feel the twisting hurt in my stomach again as I look at him, so thoroughly beaten by the sheer memory of what had happened to him.

"Show me," I say softly.

His hands tighten against his chest. "Show you…?"

"The tattoo. I want to see it."

A battle takes place in his eyes. He wants to say no, to hold his ground, but sadness and surrender tug at his strength until finally he gives in. His fingers grip his shirt, peeling it upward as slowly as if it were his own skin. The dark red whorls and lines begin to poke out at the divot between his ribs. By the time he tugs the shirt over his head, the tattoos have taken over his entire upper body. They cling to his chest with spiny symbols, reaching over his shoulders and twisting down to his elbows. They look almost alive to me. They seem to tremble with fury, as if the blood that made them is still yearning to break free, leave its prison. Luke's face doesn't belong to that thieving body.

"This is what *Stola Mortem* does," he says. "I have to live with it now. I didn't know who you were when I met you, please believe me. I would never hurt you, or your family. But there're other people that will if they find out who you are. That's what happened to Matthew."

I try to swallow and can't. It's like a hand tightens around my throat. "What do you mean?"

"*Stola Mortem* tracks down blood witches. There's not many left anymore, and even fewer people who can detect them. *Stola Mortem* has one Seer, someone like you and me who can see auras. They move constantly. It's impossible to know where they are. I didn't know they were here until they'd already killed Matthew."

The load of guilt presses down on him, pushing his shoulders forward under the weight. I want to do something to fix him, to put the pieces back together.

"My parents were in *Stola Mortem* too." The words are out before I can think.

He freezes. "What?"

"My mother and father. Emily Sayers and Faolan Sicario. My mom left when my dad went crazy. She ran away with us because she was afraid of what he'd do to us."

"That means we know each other. Or did." His fingers rest on my knee as the recognition spreads across his face. "We must have been kids together. Thousands of places we could have gone, and we ended up in the same city by accident."

"Abby thinks we can't believe in accidents anymore."

He smiles. Something sticks in his brain, drawing his eyebrows together. "Emily. There was never an Emily in the cult. Are you sure she went by that name?"

I shake my head, rubbing the stiffness in my neck.

"I don't think so." But just then, it hits me like a sheet of ice. "My mother. The 'S' is for Salem. Emily *Salem* Sayers." As soon as I say it, I know it's true. "She invented the *Veri Segno*."

Luke's hands grasp my arms, but the world tilts sideways. "Georgia. She left the cult because she didn't want to keep doing it. She wanted a new life for you." His voice trails off. "We have to find a way to keep Keir from seeing you. If he enrolls at the school, we won't be able to hide you."

"Keir, the little troll guy?" I ask.

"You've *met* him?" Alarm crackles in his tone, though he's trying hard to keep his voice level.

"He's a friend of Wyatt's."

"No, no, Georgia. Keir's my cousin, the son of my Aunt Idra." Luke grimaces. "Keir is the Seer for *Stola Mortem*. Has he seen your powers?"

"He saw one of our circles." A scalding panic rises in my chest, and I almost miss the numbness. "He's been in our house."

Luke yanks me to my feet. "Go home. Cast a circle around your house and get your sisters inside. I'm going to get Iona and meet you there."

"My sisters," I say, choking on the lump that congeals in my throat.

"They'll be fine. You're going to be fine, just be careful." He yanks the necklace off his neck, black cord with a circle of blacker stone dangling from it, and ties it roughly around my wrist. "Onyx. If there's anything that'll help you…"

Before he can finish, I clasp my hands around his neck and pull him toward me until our mouths close around each other. A weight seems to leave him, just for a second, and he presses me closer. It's the briefest moment of happiness I've had in weeks, but I know it can't last. I push back, and he lets me go.

"I take back my curse," I say, hoping it's enough of an apology.

"You have a lot of time to make it up to me," he says, pressing his thumb between my eyes, before dropping his hand, and blinking in confusion. "My spell's gone. Did you do that?"

I smile as I whip past him, desperate to get home.

As I the door closes behind me, I hear him say, "You might give them a run for their money after all."

Traps

The SUV won't move fast enough. The tires fly over the rocky asphalt, turning the scenery outside into a rushing river of grey. I get home in record time, but it still feels too late as I pull my car right up to the house, jump out, and nearly trip in my haste to get up the stairs. I slam the door behind me only to find Wyatt standing in the hall.

"You scared me. Where is everyone?" I keep some calm in my voice, not sure which Wyatt I'll get this time, my brother or the dark stranger that sometimes talks with his mouth.

"They're upstairs," he says. "What's wrong?"

I know I can't tell him, even though when I look at him now, he seems like the innocent, playful brother I'd known his whole life. For whatever reason, he'd known Keir. He'd invited him to our house. Maybe he was just as oblivious as we were, maybe Keir was using him to get close to our family, but maybe it was something else.

"Will you just start locking up the house?" I say to him. "A huge storm is coming. And tell Abby and the twins to meet me down here."

I brush past him to the kitchen, pulling Mom's box down from the pantry shelf. I toss fistfuls of rock salt and dried rosemary into the mortar and grind it, hoping it'll be enough to cover the yard. I dump the mixture into a bowl and head for the front door.

When I pass the stairs, I shout, "Everyone start locking doors and windows!" My big sister voice is back. Should be enough to get them moving.

I cast the circle from the left side of the yard to right, trying not to move too fast. It's too dark to see cars down the road, but there seems to be no one around. We just have to make it until Luke and Iona come. That's it.

Outside, a shriek splits the constant sound of cicadas. It sounds like something halfway between animal and human. I spot the owl-bird resting on the branch over my head then, her claws curving into the bark. Her eyes watch me with mild amusement before I hurl a handful of salt in her direction, making her push back from the branch with a great swat of her wings.

Back inside, our dog is having a conniption. Prince throws himself at the door to the porch, scrabbling his claws against the half-pane of glass. Wyatt appears on the stair landing, looking uneasily toward the commotion.

"Is everything locked?"

"Not the backdoor," he says.

I get to it quickly, yanking Prince back by the collar and twisting the lock. A head and shoulders step up to the glass on the other side. I reel back, nearly tripping over the dog.

Keir smiles at me through the window.

"Happy Halloween," he says.

His eyes lock on me like I'm already trapped. No way out.

"Stay away from my family, you little shark-mouthed hobbit," I spit at him.

His lips close over his teeth like curtains.

"I just came by to see Wyatt. Is the hostility really necessary?"

"We know who you are, Keir." His name comes out of my mouth as a shout. I can't hold it inside me. "Get off my porch and I won't call the police."

"Ooh, police, ooh," he mocks, leaning his hands against the glass.

I whip my head around to Wyatt, who's still frozen on the stairs.

"He can't get in, right?" I hiss at Wyatt, but he says nothing.

"Sure I can," Keir says. "Like this."

He winds up and slams the pane with a flowerpot. It sails at me in a shower of crystalline shards. I duck before it catches me in the temple.

"It's not all smoke and mirrors, you know. I can hurt you with my hands just as easily as with magic." Keir's hand snakes through the shattered hole, fingers fumbling at the lock. I throw my whole weight against the door, prying his grip off the knob.

"Wyatt, get Dad's gun!" I yell toward the stairs just as my head is ripped backward. Wyatt has a handful of my hair and is peeling me away from the door.

"What are you *doing*?" I shout, but I see them.

The dark, glassy eyes of the brother I don't know. The stranger.

"Quiet now," he says, in a voice much older than Wyatt's.

Keir steps in, and immediately a pan flies at him, followed by all the dishes in the sink. Matthew chose an excellent time to make an appearance. Keir bats them away, sucking in a breath each time they clip him.

"Come on, Matthew," he says snidely. "No hard feelings. You'll have company soon enough."

He digs in his pockets, pulling out a vial that he empties into his hands. He rubs them together and places his palms on the wall, closing his eyes to say a garbled spell before stepping back. A satisfied smile twists up the corners of his mouth.

The pipes above our heads begin to moan and creak so fiercely that I think the ceiling might collapse, but whatever Keir's done has trapped Matthew.

Wyatt drags me backward, making sure not to give me an inch of room to struggle. We stumble into the living room as Keir pushes furniture back, exposing the wooden floor beneath.

"Who are you?" I demand of the stranger wearing Wyatt's face. "What do you want?"

His sigh blows cold across the top of my head. "I did hope something in you would know me. I remember you best of all. You were my favorite."

Paralysis grips my body. It's like I'm trapped under ice, to cold to move. I do know that voice. It's been a lifetime, but I feel it in my bones.

"You're Faolan," I say. "You're my father."

Before he can answer, there's commotion on the stairs. Someone's dropped something big. Thinking my sisters are still in their rooms, I twist in Wyatt's grasp and yell to them.

"Get out of the house! Go get Gemmie!"

From under Wyatt's arm, I see a woman descend the stairs. She's tugging Abby by the wrists. My sister's limp body bumps over each step like a dragged doll. The woman heaves her the short distance into the living room, letting Abby's head smack the ground when she drops her. The woman turns to me then, and I know exactly where I've seen that same sharp nose, those penetrating blue eyes set in caramel skin. It couldn't be anyone else. Luke's mother smiles at me the way a tiger might smile and it's so familiar it makes me shiver.

"We've waited a long time," she says to my father.

"Death takes none of us, Isolda," he says, an old fondness in his voice.

She smiles, her mouth so like Luke's it stirs up bile in my stomach.

"Death takes none of us," she repeats. Her gaze ticks to me. "Georgia. All grown up."

She runs a long finger down my cheek as she speaks. I kick out at her, and get a punch to the skull from Faolan that rattles my brain.

She doesn't even blink at my outburst. "I wondered when I'd see you again. Your mother and I had such plans for you and Luke. It's only fitting you spent your last months together."

"What'd you do to my sister?" I demand through clenched teeth.

Isolda doesn't even look at her, just purses her lips. "Don't worry, she's rather simply spelled. We need her alive for now."

As soon as she says it, two men emerge from upstairs. They're hauling Callie and Charlotte down behind them. On the stairs, my sisters put up more of a fight than I did. Callie tears at the shoulder of her captor with her long nails. He's got a greasy ponytail and a vacant face, someone I wouldn't look twice at out on the street. But when he looks at Isolda, a sickening light fills his eyes, like he'd do anything for her.

Charlotte has an open cut in the middle of her forehead, but she's still clamping her teeth down on any exposed skin she can find. I recognize her kidnapper as the scrawny shopkeeper from Oggun. When they reach the living room, the twins are dropped heavily on the ground. It's then that I see what Keir's been working on. The living room floor is one huge casting circle, symbols layered over symbols with thick white chalk.

Isolda gathers her glossy black hair into a braid like a runner before a race. "Come now, sweet thing," she says to me. "We have a long night ahead of us."

Sacrifice

There are five of them, including Wyatt's puppet master. Each member takes a point of the gigantic pentagram, the outlying mark on the floor. When they close the circle, the house moans and the floorboards seem to rock like a boat in a storm, making me sick. I curl forward on the floor, locking my head against my knees. The shopkeeper stands directly behind me, and by the way Charlotte stares daggers at him, he's responsible for the gash on her forehead. Abby is still unconscious, her head in Callie's lap.

One thought presses down on my whole body: Luke, his aunt, his uncle — *they're not going to get here in time.*

I fix my eyes on Wyatt's, trying to pull my baby brother out with my stare. It's useless. Faolan hadn't had him this whole time. But at some point, Wyatt had wrestled his own mind back, had forced Faolan out. He was strong enough to do it again. I knew it.

But only Faolan stares back at me, cold and glazed. It strikes me that Wyatt must look like him. I feel stupid for not noticing before. He never had Mom's heart-shaped face, or the thin nose we all shared. Faolan ticks his head to the side, trying to puzzle out what I'm thinking.

"What kind of man kills his own children for power?" I growl. It doesn't even sound like my voice.

The armor cracks. He drops his half-sneer, paling a bit.

"You were never my children," he says breezily. "You were tools."

"Liar. You were afraid of us." Fury boils in my chest, roiling up into my throat. "You knew we'd be more powerful than you. And you knew she loved us more than you. You're a coward."

Movement flashes across my vision as Isolda's hand smashes me across the cheek.

"Do not speak to the Prophet like that!" She spits when she says it.

"*Prophet?*" I press my hand against my stinging face. "He's a psychopath. You're *all* psychopaths. We're children!" I yell at her, the sound raking my throat.

From her pocket, she pulls out a smoothed red stone the size of her palm. She whispers words in Spanish, breathing on it, then presses it over my heart.

My skin ripples under the burn that spreads from the stone as pain punches into my chest, setting my heart on fire. I scream, trying to pry her hands away, but she pushes me backward onto the floor, holding me down with her left hand. With her right, she raises a dagger over my head, the point hovering between my eyes. My limbs seize up one joint at a time, elbows, knees, hips, until I can do nothing but let the pain split my ribs apart.

As Isolda begins to chant, the room stands still.

"*Our God of fire, we call you.*

Take this body, this blood, these bones,
And return to us the soul of our Prophet to the body we choose.
Take our payment and make him whole—"

"No!" Callie throws herself on Isolda's arm, snatching at the dagger. The two pitch backward, and Isolda's hand comes off the stone in my chest. Cool air rushes into my lungs, extinguishing the fire. Even without the stone, the circle still makes me feel like I'm in an over-pressurized container, anchoring me to the ground. It's a wonder Callie can move.

I force myself to sit up, roll onto my knees so I can help her, but it's too late. Keir wrestles her off his aunt, pinning her arms behind her. Callie goes limp, and I know she's spent all of her energy saving me.

I try to pull myself over to her just as the front door slams open, breathing air into the house. Luke and Iona sprint into the living room, pulling up just before the circle.

"Sister," Iona says, her jaw set in pure hatred, "let the children go. The police are on their way."

Still recovering from the tussle with Callie, Isolda lifts herself to one knee and the animal smile returns to her face as she bares sharp white teeth. "Oh, I think they'll have some trouble getting here. Perhaps a little water on the road."

"Oh, we saw that," Iona says with the tiniest hint of a smirk. "You really should know better than to use water magic against your son."

That sets Isolda back a tick. Behind her, I see the bony shopkeeper from Oggun sweating, trying to gauge how much of a shot he has against Luke. He decides to make a run for it, darting for the open door. Luke intercepts him there and downs him with a left hook before spinning on his heel, reaching deep into his pocket, and bringing up a closed fist.

He holds his hand to his mouth, like his mother had done, and speaks a fast string of Spanish into it. Without warning, he flings his hand forward, scattering white powder over the heart of the circle.

Right then the pressure lifts, freeing us.

"Get out of the circle!" he shouts at me.

Charlotte and I snap to it, flipping Abby over and grabbing her shirt on either side to pull her away. Greasy Ponytail cuts right past us, heading for Luke. He has a look of righteous fury on his face. It's obvious that, son or not, Luke has gotten in Isolda's way, and Ponytail figures he's going to put a stop to it. When he reaches Luke, he doesn't bother with punches. He goes straight for the throat.

Charlotte and I have almost got Abby to the far side of the room. As soon as we're out of the circle, I set her down as gently as I can and turn back, heading for Luke.

"Isolda!" Faolan bellows over the commotion. "I'm not losing this body!"

Isolda brings her arm back, then whips it forward, fingers aimed at me. I don't even see the dagger, I just feel a punch in my gut. It's only when I look down that I see the thing, buried up to its hilt in my stomach.

Purge

I'm laying on my side, watching the spreading red puddle overtake white symbols on the floor. My thoughts come slower now, like my brain is lagging behind my breathing. I try to run through a list of spells, but not one of them can help me. Outside the circle, Callie cries and Charlotte's eyes lock on me as she positions herself protectively over Ally. She only flinches a little as Iona rushes past her, taking four quick strides to Wyatt and throwing a handful of salt directly into his eyes.

It wouldn't have hurt a normal person much, but Wyatt's possessed body lets out a wail that breaks my heart. He paws at his face while something like smoke curls up from his skin. He sinks to his knees, and Iona kicks him to the ground. Quick as a cat, she pulls a pair of silver scissors from her pocket and splits his shirt so his back shines in the light. Every inch of skin is tattooed over with a net of symbols.

Iona holds a cross to her forehead, speaking in a rush of Spanish. She leans forward, pressing the cross against

Wyatt's back. He writhes under it, every muscle tensing and twitching at once and the tattoos *move*. They squirm and twist like snakes, turning black as if they're dying in his skin.

That's when the police bust in. They pour through the front door, fanning out through the room. What's left of *Stola Mortem* bolts in two opposite directions. Isolda runs right past me, and I glare at her with all the hatred I've ever felt, imagining my hands closing around her ankles.

She trips. It's only for a moment, but she whips back to me, her eyes wide. I blink, just as surprised as she is. As an officer moves for her, she turns from me, her black hair flying behind her as she tears past the policemen and out the front door. They're after her in a flash, swarming like bees.

Faolan meets my eyes, still prone across the floor, his face is pink with fresh burns. He's so pale. His head jerks from side to side, but whatever Iona did has taken any power he had.

"She's ruined it," he says. "She ruined the seal."

The prickling beginnings of numbness take over my left arm. When I lift it out of the wetness, the black stone on my wrist bumps against my palm, like a cat wanting to be petted. I hold it up, peering at the dark beauty of it.

If he hadn't been a foot from my face, I would have missed it. But I see the stab of fear in Faolan's eyes when he sees the onyx. I can't explain why, but my hand closes around the amulet. I summon the last strand of strength in my body and rise onto my elbow.

"Give me back my brother," I say, and push the stone against his forehead.

Onyx

It smells like Lysol. I open my eyes, wondering who's cleaning my room so early in the morning, but instead of seeing my ceiling, I'm staring at white industrial tiles and rectangular fluorescent lights.

It's a hospital. I try to sit up, but my stomach gives me a sharp warning not to.

"Georgia?" Luke leans into my sightline, his hand on my shoulder.

"I got stabbed," I tell him.

He laughs his breathy laugh. "I know. You got a lot of stitches, but you're okay. I'm going to call your family."

"I'm going to go back to sleep," I say, but my eyelids have already made the decision for me. His lips press against my cheek. It's the last feeling I get before I spiral down into blackness.

I don't see her, but I feel her. Gemmie's hand rests on mine, her touch cool on my burning skin. The rim of something hard and ceramic bumps against my lower lip.

"Darling, drink this. It's going to help you get through this more quickly."

I take a gulp of the tepid liquid, tasting faint chamomile and something sweet.

"Is it going to heal me?" I ask. My voice could be coming from a different body, it sounds so low and gritty.

There's a heavy pause. Gemmie smoothes the hair off my face, tucking it behind my ears.

"Even I can't do that, my heart. I can just give you a little comfort to pass the time. It makes your mind very open, so try to be aware who's around you."

Two of her fingers settle between my eyes, and she whispers a quick chant. The weight that's been pressing me into the sheets leaves me. My mind whirls with color and images, and I sink into them.

Our old house stands in front of me, still towering in its Victorian height, not a single singed board. I walk toward it, feeling the lush grass under my feet. The front door opens, and she steps out to meet me.

My mother, exactly as I remember her. Her red hair is pulled to the side of her neck in a thick braid. Her feet are bare as she stops in front of me, tipping my chin up with her smooth fingers. Her jade eyes warm when they meet mine, filling with that laughing light like they always did.

"Mom?" I say.

Dark clouds move across her face, the corners of her mouth falling just slightly. She opens her mouth to say something.

"Georgia?" It's not my mom's voice.

The world swims into focus again. Wyatt's sitting in the chair beside my hospital bed. Despite my bandages and the doctor's orders not to move, I almost shy away. But when he looks at me, I see my brother. I see only hurt and sadness. The lingering evil and the hardness it brought with it is gone. Now he's a sickly yellow color, with circles under his eyes so dark he looks like he has two black eyes.

"You look as bad as I feel," I croak.

He smiles sadly before saying, "Iona said you saved me."

"Iona saved you."

"You took him out though." Wyatt's voice cracks. "You drew his soul out."

I touch my wrist, remembering the onyx stone. It's gone, along with the cord that held it.

"I guess I did," I say slowly. "Wyatt. Why didn't you tell us? How could you keep it from me?"

He lets his face fall into his hands. "It was the voices again. I was hearing them everywhere, telling me someone was looking for me, that we were all in danger. You and I are the only ones that get omens, you know what it can be like. I felt like I was losing my mind. Then Keir just showed up out of nowhere and said he knew what was going on. That I wasn't crazy. That he could help me. It was just small stuff at first. We practiced in the woods by our house, and he knew so much."

"The circle," I say. "I've been there. That was you and Keir?"

He nods. "But I wanted to do what he could do. He could *move* things, make people do what he wanted. He said he could make it so I could do it too."

He tells me the story of the fire, the remnants of Gemmie's spell painting the picture in my mind.

"Keir tricked me," he says. "He told me we were doing the *Veri Segno*, but he was just using Matthew as an offering. He sealed Faolan's soul in me." He swallows roughly. "Doesn't feel right calling him Dad, does it?"

"You should have told us," I say, my voice rasping under the strain of holding myself together.

"Told you what? That I helped *kill* a person? Matthew was my age. Just a guy. When you pushed me into the circle, we raised something from his blood. I'm responsible for that, for the fact that he's still not moved on."

"Wyatt, I know you. And you are a *good* person. We'll find a way to make it right."

He leans over, resting his head on the bed next to me. I run my fingers over his hair, the way Mom used to do.

"What happened to the cult members?" I ask. "Did the police catch them all?"

The thought of them doing prison time gives me just enough satisfaction that I don't think about the ache in my stomach for a moment.

"They got the two guys. Keir and Isolda got away."

"That's not possible. I *saw* them chase Isolda, they had her."

He shrugs, looking exhausted. "They said they lost her. She just vanished."

"There's just no way she could've gotten away," I say, massaging my forehead. She was right *there*.

The image of her face, those merciless watching eyes, burns behind my eyelids. My head snaps up. All this time, I thought the familiarity I saw was because of Luke, but I had been seeing that face for a month. It had been staring down at me from trees.

Lechuza. The word the old woman outside of Oggun had hissed into my memory. Finally I remember what the name means. *Lechuza*, the witch-bird. It was one of the stories Mom used to tell us when we first moved to Texas. The *brujas* in West Texas who turn themselves into giant birds. But it hadn't been real. It couldn't be real.

"I can't believe you get to miss school," Abby says, sinking down onto my bed.

I shove a corner of grilled cheese into my mouth.

"I'm traumatized," I say happily.

"So am I! I went through it too."

"You were spelled. You slept through the whole thing," I say, closing Mom's journal and setting it on my dresser. "Don't get too jealous, though. It's not like Dad's ever going to let me out of his sight again."

"Small price." Abby stands up, fluffing out her skirt. "Do you want to watch a movie tonight?"

"Sure," I say, touching soreness in my stomach. It's almost healed, just feels like a pulled muscle most of the time. "Luke's coming over after school, we can all hang out together."

She wrinkles her nose. "No, y'all are weird with your PDA."

She flounces out of the room, waving as she closes the door. I open my Chem book, wanting to start the horrible process of catching up. A soft knock interrupts me.

Wyatt is standing in my doorway.

"Oh," I stammer. "Hey."

"I have something that I think belongs to you," he says.

The onyx stone dangles from his finger.

"Wyatt, you found it." I get up, taking it from him.

"I didn't lose it. I just didn't know what to do with it." He breathes out. "I think a part of me liked having him around. Like he'd kind of become part of me. I can't explain it."

"What do you mean?"

He taps the stone. "Look into it."

I hold it closer, peering into the dark heart of it. Only it isn't dark anymore. What had once been a dead reflection now roils with an angry red glow.

"What is it?" I say.

Wyatt cocks his head. He says, "You can't feel it?"

I shrug.

Wyatt takes the stone, resting it in his palm so the red light dances against his skin.

"It's him," he says. "This is Faolan Sicario's *soul*."

Kate was born in a tiny town outside of Austin, TX. At fourteen, she was accepted to a creative writing summer program at Oxford University in England. After attending a creative arts boarding school Kate worked her way over to California to study creative writing at Chapman University. When not writing, she's teaching children to not fall off horses. *Spelled* is the first novella in a series.

Ryan Gattis is a writer, curator, and creative writing professor at Chapman University. He holds an M.A. in Fiction Writing from the University of East Anglia in Norwich, England, and is the author of novels *Roo Kickkick & the Big Bad Blimp* and *Kung Fu High School*, which was acquired by The Weinstein Company. In 2012, he wrote and curated the story-driven art show "The Art of Kung Fu: Myths and Legends" and works closely with street art collective UGLAR (uglarworks.com) as Narrative Director on various public art projects. Raised in Colorado, he lives in Downtown Los Angeles.

Davide Bonazzi lives in Bologna (Italy), where he was born in 1984. After he graduated from the University of Bologna, Faculty of Arts and Humanities, he studied Illustration in Milan at IED – European Institute of Design and at the Academy of Fine Arts of Bologna. Since 2008 he works as a freelance illustrator. Among his clients, *The Boston Globe*, *The Wall Street Journal*, *Scientific American*, *Columbia Magazine*, Hachette Books, Timberland, Greenpeace, L'Espresso and many others.

Made in the USA
Lexington, KY
03 November 2014